Garry Hede

THE MYSTERY AT DEVIL'S PAW

The HARDY BOYS *Mystery Stories*
BY FRANKLIN W. DIXON

"There's something in here?" Frank cried out

"There's something in here!" Frank cried out

Hardy Boys Mystery Stories

THE MYSTERY

AT

DEVIL'S PAW

BY

FRANKLIN W. DIXON

NEW YORK
GROSSET & DUNLAP
Publishers

*The author proudly dedicates this book
to the boys and girls of Alaska,
which became our forty-ninth state
during the writing of*
THE MYSTERY AT DEVIL'S PAW

CONTENTS

CHAPTER I

Highway Attack

"TELEGRAM for Frank and Joe Hardy!"

The messenger gave an envelope to the seventeen-year-old, blond-haired boy who answered the door at the Hardys' home in Bayport. Joe signed for it and hurried into the living room.

"Who's it from?" asked Frank Hardy excitedly. The dark-haired boy, a year older than Joe, waited patiently while his brother slit the envelope and took out the telegram.

"It's from Tony!" Joe exclaimed.

Tony Prito, a good friend of the Hardy boys, had gone to Alaska the week before to take a summer job as stream guard with the Fish and Wildlife Service. The two brothers eagerly read the night letter:

BELIEVE I HAVE STUMBLED ON A WEIRD
MYSTERY. MY LIFE MAY BE IN DANGER.
TRY TO COME RIGHT AWAY AND BRING

CHET MORTON. WHEN YOU ARRIVE JU-
NEAU ASK FOR TED SEWELL AT SEAPLANE
DOCK.

"Jumping catfish!" Joe exclaimed. "It sounds urgent!"

"Tony must be in real trouble," Frank agreed, frowning. "I sure hope Mom and Dad will let us go."

Fenton Hardy, the boys' father, had been a famous detective on the New York City police force. After retiring and moving to Bayport, the tall, athletic-looking sleuth had gained even more renown as a private investigator. Frank and Joe, who had inherited their father's zeal for bringing criminals to justice, often helped him unravel his cases.

The two boys hurried out to the garden in back of the house, where Mr. and Mrs. Hardy were seated on lawn chairs, enjoying the afternoon sunshine. Gertrude Hardy, the boys' tall, thin maiden aunt, was serving glasses of iced tea.

"Dad!" Joe cried excitedly. "May Frank and I go to Alaska?"

"Just like that?" Fenton Hardy chuckled. "Sit down and tell us what this is all about."

"Humph!" put in Aunt Gertrude. "Sounds like another mystery to me. I can always tell the symptoms! You'll freeze to death in Alaska. Mark my words!"

"Oh, Auntie!" Joe exclaimed. "Alaska isn't all ice and snow. A few days ago it was eighty degrees in Juneau."

"Seems incredible," Mr. Hardy agreed, "but it's true. The Alaskan Panhandle has weather much like Washington or Oregon, with plenty of rain."

"Then you'll both get wet and die of pneumonia!" Aunt Gertrude went on, not to be deterred.

The brothers suppressed a smile as the conversation about the new state continued. Only the far north was frigid, Joe recalled from his geography lessons. He even remembered that Alaska was an Aleut Indian name meaning "The Great Land," and was also referred to as the "Crossroads of the World."

"And we can't leave Tony stranded at the crossroads," Frank pleaded. He showed his father the telegram.

Fenton Hardy scanned the message, reflected a moment, then passed it to his wife. "What do you think, Laura?"

Mrs. Hardy, a slim, pretty woman, read the telegram with a slight frown. "It sounds rather dangerous."

"Of course it's dangerous!" Aunt Gertrude had adjusted her spectacles so as to read the telegram over Mrs. Hardy's shoulder. "Alaska is full of man-killing bears and treacherous glaciers," she warned. "And besides, I heard a rumor on the newscast last week that a United States rocket intended for the moon dropped in Alaska!"

"But what's that got to do with our helping Tony?" Frank asked.

"It could happen again!" Miss Hardy retorted in a peppery tone.

"Boy, that would make our trip even more exciting!" Joe said, his eyes twinkling mischievously.

Aunt Gertrude sighed deeply. "Won't you boys ever take my advice?" she fumed.

After a moment's thought, Mrs. Hardy said, "I'll leave the decision to your father."

The tall, broad-shouldered detective smiled as Frank asked eagerly, "Could we take your plane, Dad?"

Under the direction of Jack Wayne, Mr. Hardy's pilot, both Frank and Joe had become experts at piloting the six-place, single-engine craft which their father had recently purchased.

"I'm afraid not, son," Mr. Hardy replied. "I need it myself. Jack is flying me to Miami to wind up an investigation." Mr. Hardy looked at his sons quizzically. "It'll cost quite a bit to fly to Alaska on the regular airlines."

"We've thought of that, Dad," Frank responded. "Joe and I have saved several hundred dollars from odd jobs. We were putting it aside for an outboard motor."

"But Tony comes first!" Joe added stoutly.

The detective was impressed by his sons' loyalty to their friend, and said so. "All right, you have the go-ahead from me, boys. I'll chip in with a few more dollars if you need it!"

"Great, Dad!" Frank pumped his father's hand, while Joe, seized with enthusiasm, waltzed his mother around until she protested that she was getting dizzy.

Jubilant, the boys telephoned Chet Morton. Chet, a stocky, good-natured boy, was the Hardys' friend and classmate at Bayport High.

"I'll ask my folks if I can go along, too," their chum replied after hearing the news.

"Well, make it snappy!" Frank urged. "We'll have to get plane reservations right away."

Chet promised to let them know his parents' decision as soon as possible and hung up.

Twenty minutes later Chet's noisy jalopy chugged up in front of the Hardys' pleasant, tree-shaded home. The brothers ran out to view the high-sprung and topless car, which gleamed with a fresh coat of red paint.

"How do you like it?" Chet said proudly as he climbed down out of the front seat.

"Good night," Joe groaned. "What museum did you buy *that* from?"

"Museum!" Chet glared and wiped the perspiration from his chubby face. "Listen, this baby can really roll!"

"Okay, but how about the trip to Alaska?" Frank asked. "Can you come?"

Chet looked worried. "It's okay with my folks, but—well, I'm not sure I ought to go."

"Why not?" Joe demanded. "If Tony's in trouble, you want to help him, don't you?"

"Sure, but that's just it—the *danger*," Chet replied nervously. "How do I know we won't get plugged by gold thieves or someone? Last time I took a trip with you fellows, I got chained in an underground dungeon!"

Chet referred to their recent adventure in Puerto Rico, where the Hardy boys had tracked down an international ring of lawbreakers responsible for *The Ghost at Skeleton Rock.*

"Stop worrying." Frank chuckled. "Think of the salmon fishing in Alaska! Can't you visualize a nice plump Chinook salmon sizzling on the fire?"

"Mm, boy!" Chet immediately perked up. "Well, okay. We can't let Tony down!"

"That's the spirit," said Joe, slapping the stout boy on the back. "Let's phone for plane reservations!"

The three hurried inside and stood by while Frank dialed the airport ticket office. "Line's busy," he announced impatiently.

After trying for several minutes without success to contact the airport, the Hardys decided to drive there.

"We can take my new hotrod," Chet offered. "It'll get us out there in a jiffy!"

"In one piece?" Frank asked, winking at Joe.

"Hop aboard!" Chet commanded.

When the trio had squeezed in, he threw the car into gear and started off with a roar.

Soon they were rolling along the highway toward the airport. When they reached the flight terminal, Frank asked the clerk at the ticket counter for three reservations to Juneau, Alaska.

"How soon do you want to leave?" the clerk inquired.

"Tomorrow morning, if possible."

The clerk shook his head. "Sorry, but we're booked solid for a week as far as Chicago. That's where you'll make flight connections."

The boys looked at each other in dismay. "Is travel heavy?" Frank asked.

"Well, not exactly," the clerk replied. "In the past few days, several passengers who made reservations didn't show up for their flights. In fact, they haven't even been around to ask for refunds on their tickets."

"If any other passengers don't show up," Joe queried, "can we take their places?"

"Certainly, if you're standing by at flight time. But, you understand, I can't guarantee accommodations."

After a hasty conference the boys accepted this arrangement. "If we can't get space in the next twenty-four hours, let's hop a train or bus," Frank suggested.

Joe and Chet both agreed to this. As they

turned away from the counter, Joe gave his brother a slight nudge.

"What's up?" Frank asked quietly.

"Take a look at that man next to the water cooler. He's been listening to everything we said."

The stranger, dark-haired and with piercing eyes, seemed to realize that the boys were talking about him. Hastily he walked away and strode out the front door of the terminal.

"Who was he?" asked Chet.

"Search me," Joe replied. "Maybe he was just nosy, but he might have had a reason for eavesdropping on us."

Hurrying out of the building, the boys looked around, but the man had disappeared.

The trio climbed into the jalopy and headed back toward Bayport, with Chet clinging to the wheel like a racing driver.

"Okay, Barney Oldfield," Joe teased him. "Give it more gas or we'll be arrested for holding up traffic."

Glancing at his rear-view mirror, Chet remarked, "That truck in back of us certainly is highballing."

Frank and Joe turned their heads to see a large black vehicle approaching them, exceeding the speed limit.

"Give that cowboy plenty of room to pass," Frank said.

"Right." Chet drove closer to the side of the

road, only inches from the edge of a ditch which separated the highway from a strip of wooded land.

With the roar of the truck directly behind him, Chet gave the signal to pass. Suddenly he looked to his left and exclaimed, "Hey, stop crowding me!"

"Look out there!" Joe cried. The truck's cab was so high that he could not see the driver.

The next instant the side of the passing truck brushed Chet's jalopy. With a sickening scraping sound and the shriek of rubber against pavement, the boys' car tumbled into the ditch, coming to rest on its side.

Seconds later, stunned from the accident, the Hardys crawled clear of the car. The truck was out of sight.

"O-oh, my head!" Joe groaned as he struggled to collect his wits. Chet lay grotesquely over the wheel, his eyes closed.

The brothers eased their friend gently from the jalopy. While they were trying to revive him, several passing motorists stopped to offer assistance.

"I'll call the police," a woman promised. "There should be a phone at the next gas station."

In a matter of minutes, a state police car arrived at the scene and two officers got out. Chet was just regaining consciousness.

"Need an ambulance?" one of the troopers asked.

"N-no, I'm okay," Chet said woozily. "But I sure feel sore all over!"

Frank and Joe reported the accident to the officers. "That guy must have a grudge against us. He deliberately forced us into the ditch!" Joe said hotly.

"Could be," the troopers commented. "Did you get the license number?"

"No, sir. It all happened too fast," Frank replied glumly, but he gave a complete description of the vehicle.

"Our men will be on the lookout for it," the older officer said, and added, "We'll help pull your buggy back on the road." After they had done this, a wrecker towed Chet's car to a garage.

The troopers, meanwhile, insisted on driving the boys to Bayport Hospital. A doctor examined them, and after bandaging a cut on Chet's head, suggested that the stout youth rest in bed until fully recovered. Miraculously, the Hardy boys were unharmed, except for some minor bruises.

Chet was driven to the Morton farm. Then Frank and Joe accompanied the officers to Bayport Police Headquarters. After hearing their story, Chief Collig, an old friend of the Hardys, asked:

"Any idea who might be responsible?"

Frank shook his head. "Not unless someone is

The passing truck brushed Chet's jalopy

trying to keep us from going to Alaska." He explained about Tony Prito's telegram and the eavesdropper at the airport.

"Well," said Chief Collig, "our prowl cars and the state police will keep looking for that truck."

When they arrived home, the Hardys told their father privately of what had happened. Mr. Hardy looked grave. "I'm afraid this proves that you're up against a nasty enemy," he commented. "Better not mention the attack to your mother or Aunt Gertrude."

Frank and Joe went to bed that night sobered by the thought that they were tackling a dangerous case. And what about Tony? Was he still safe —or had he, too, met with some kind of "accident"?

The next morning, however, the brothers were heartened by an early telephone call from Chet Morton, who said that he had completely recovered from his head injury. After eating breakfast and packing their clothes, Frank and Joe said good-by to their family and drove to the airport in their yellow convertible.

"If we get on the plane," Frank said, "we'll just leave the car in the parking lot until we get back."

While taking their luggage out of the trunk, they saw Chet pull into the lot. Apparently his jalopy, though scratched and dented, was still roadworthy. Beside him sat two pretty girls.

"Hey! Iola and Callie!" Joe shouted.

"We came to see you off," said Chet's dark-haired sister, Iola Morton.

"I was hoping you might," Joe admitted with a grin.

"Ditto!" Frank said, smiling at his own favorite date, Callie Shaw.

"Don't get lost in that Alaskan wilderness," warned Callie, an attractive blonde with sparkling brown eyes.

"We'll try not to. Sure you're feeling okay, Chet?"

"Fit as a fiddle!"

The boys checked in at the ticket counter, then said good-by to the girls who left in Chet's car to keep a tennis date.

At ten o'clock the boys lined up at the outside gate as the Chicago-bound plane landed and taxied up to the airport building.

"Hey, look!" Joe whispered to his companions. "There's that man again!"

The stranger who had eavesdropped the day before was pacing nervously up and down, apparently unaware of the Hardys. As he strode past, Frank pointed to his footprint in the dirt. The heelmark showed a circle with a star in it.

Moments later, the loading ramp was wheeled up to the big airliner and the passengers streamed aboard. A voice over the public-address system began paging the Hardys, so the boys hurried back to check at the ticket counter.

"Two empty seats," the airline clerk told them.

The Hardys and Chet stared at one another in a quandary. If they accepted the seats, one of the trio would have to be left behind.

As they pondered, the suspicious stranger rushed angrily to the counter. "Now wait a minute!" he challenged. "Those seats were paid for by friends of mine. You have no right to assign them to someone else!"

"Oh, yes, we do," the clerk retorted. "If your friends aren't on hand for the flight, they can ask for refunds later." Turning back to the boys, he added, "How about it?"

"B-b-but there's three of us!" Chet stuttered.

"You'll have to make up your minds, boys," the clerk said. "I can't wait any longer."

CHAPTER II

Decoy

FRANK solved the dilemma with a quick decision. "Suppose I stay here and catch the next available plane. Joe, you and Chet go on and wait for me at Chicago."

Chet volunteered to remain but was overruled.

"Okay, Frank. Good luck," Joe said.

As the stranger stood by, glowering, Chet and Joe purchased their tickets and rushed out to the gate. At the loading ramp a stewardess was helping a woman out of the plane.

The passenger was trembling and wrought up. "I can't do it!" she sobbed. "I won't go! Imagine treating three nice boys that way!"

"Good grief!" Joe whispered. "Does she mean us?"

Before Chet could comment, the dark-haired man rushed up.

"Not him again!" Joe muttered. The boys

15

looked on, amazed, as the man grabbed the woman's arm and snapped to the stewardess, "Have her bags taken off the plane!" Then he marched the sobbing woman back to the airport building.

"That'll mean another empty space!" Chet exclaimed. "We'd better tell Frank!"

But Frank, who had been standing at the gate, had sized up the situation and dashed back to the airline counter. A moment later, grinning and clutching his ticket, he sprinted to the plane.

"I made it!" he exclaimed.

The boys went up the ramp, stepped inside the plane, and took their seats. Luckily, the three were able to sit together. There was a brief wait while the boys' suitcases were loaded aboard. Then, after taxiing into position, the airliner roared down the runway and took off.

"Frank, what about that woman?" Joe asked as he unfastened his seat belt a few minutes later. "Think she was referring to us?"

"She must have been," Frank replied. "We're the only boys on board."

"But what did she mean by that remark about 'treating three nice boys that way'?"

Frank shrugged, frowning. "The whole thing seems fishy to me. I have a hunch, Joe, that we'd better be extra-cautious for the rest of this flight."

To the Hardys' relief, however, the first leg of the trip proved to be uneventful. The plane landed at Chicago, where the boys had a twenty-five-minute wait. Then, after boarding the Seattle flight, they winged across the prairie states and the Rocky Mountains.

It was brisk and cool when they landed at Seattle–Tacoma airport. Frank, Joe, and Chet strolled into the airport waiting room.

Glancing at the wall clock, Frank remarked, "An hour to go before we board the plane for Juneau."

"Man alive, we sure made good time!" Chet gasped. "It's only one forty-seven."

"Don't forget that we gained three hours flying west," Joe reminded him with a chuckle.

"Look, fellows," Frank put in, "I think I should call Dad and tell him what happened back at Bayport just before we took off. He might be able to check on that man and woman."

A row of telephone booths lined one wall of the waiting room. Frank stepped into one and put through a long-distance call to the Hardy residence. Much to Frank's amazement, Fenton Hardy knew all about the Bayport episode.

"I drove out to the airport to see if you boys had taken off yet," Mr. Hardy explained. "I reached the outside gate just as you were embarking. The guard, Dick Harper, is a friend of mine. He told me about that woman making a fuss and getting off the plane. The man who grabbed her looked familiar, so I played a hunch and followed them."

"Did you find out who he was?" Frank asked eagerly.

"Yes—a wanted spy named Romo Stransky," the detective replied. "I had him arrested and quizzed the woman."

The latter, Mr. Hardy related, turned out to be the owner of a boardinghouse where Stransky had been staying. She was frightened and said that Stransky had bought her a flight ticket to Chicago and paid her an extra fifty dollars to make the trip.

"Why didn't she go through with it?" asked Frank.

"She heard him telling someone over an airport phone that he had reserved all the unsold seats in order to keep three boys from going to Chicago. Later on, after boarding the plane, she got very worried and went all to pieces. Thought there might be something crooked involved and didn't want to get mixed up in it."

Frank chuckled. "Looks as though Stransky outsmarted himself that time."

"He certainly did," Mr. Hardy agreed. "Incidentally, I found out that he posed as a travel agent in order to buy up all those blocks of seats to Chicago."

"Dad, he must have planned on having two of his friends aboard that plane this morning," Frank pointed out. "That's probably why Joe and I were able to get seats."

"No doubt you're right, son. The question now is what is behind all this. Stransky won't talk, but you boys may be in real danger. Be careful!"

"We'll watch our step, Dad," Frank promised. "And give our love to Mother and Aunt Gertrude."

After hanging up, Frank stepped out of the booth. Joe was waiting outside. They saw Chet running toward them with a wild-eyed look.

"Hey, fellows, guess what! The guy we saw in Bayport this morning! He's here at this airport!"

"That's impossible, Chet," Frank declared. "Dad had him arrested!" Hastily Frank reported his telephone conversation with Mr. Hardy.

"Then Stransky must have a double," Chet insisted, "because the man I saw was a dead-ringer for him!"

"Where did you spot him?" Frank asked.

"Right over there by the magazine stand." As Chet turned to point, his eyes widened in surprise. "He's gone!"

"Come on! Maybe we can still find him!" Joe urged.

The three boys made a fast circuit of the building. They also checked the parking lot and the outside gates that led to the flight apron. But Stransky's double was nowhere in sight.

"What a way to start this trip!" Chet wailed.

"Here I was just going along for some nice salmon fishing. Now you've got me all mixed up with a bunch of spies and even seeing double!"

"Cheer up," Joe said. "You leave the spies to us, and we'll still get in some fishing!"

Within an hour, a voice boomed out over the loud-speaker, "Flight for Juneau, Alaska, now loading at Gate Ten!"

The three boys trooped aboard the huge clipper plane with the other passengers and fastened their seat belts. Minutes later, they were soaring high above the Pacific coast.

After winging high over Vancouver Island, the clipper flew steadily northward up the rugged Canadian coast. Majestic green-clad mountains towered up to snowy peaks, and the blue waters offshore were dotted with rocky islands.

"Boy, what vacation country!" Frank said enthusiastically.

Even Chet was now relaxed. "I'm sure glad that Tony sent for us," he said, beaming.

Favorable tail winds speeded their trip, and in a few hours the boys sighted Juneau. The city lay nestled at the foot of a steep mountain. A bridge connected it with Douglas Island across narrow Gastineau Channel.

"Where do we land?" Chet wondered aloud.

His question was answered a few minutes later as the plane came down on an airfield several miles to the north.

From here, they were whisked by car back to Juneau along the beautiful Glacier Highway. Frank and Joe watched, but noticed no one trailing them. Soon the forested slopes of the mountain gave way to the outskirts of town.

"Jeepers, it's a real city," Chet remarked, eying the modern buildings.

"What did you expect—log cabins?" Joe chuckled. "This *is* the capital of Alaska."

The airport car stopped and unloaded in front of a white building.

"Baranof Hotel," the driver explained proudly.

Chet whistled in amazement as they entered the attractive lobby of the modern hotel.

"Boy, I sure never expected anything like this in Alaska!"

As soon as the bellhop had taken them to their rooms, Chet sank down on his comfortable bed. "Think I'll catch forty winks," he yawned. "That meal on the plane made me sleepy."

The Hardys grinned. "Okay," Joe said. "Frank and I will look up Ted Sewell."

Chet's heavy breathing indicated that he had drifted off to sleep even before the Hardys had unpacked their luggage.

"Well, Chet's in good country for sawing logs," Frank quipped quietly as the brothers slipped on sweaters and left the room.

At the desk in the lobby Joe asked directions to

the seaplane dock. It was a five-minute walk.
When the boys arrived there they were surprised
to see a huge floating dock which lay low in the
water. Two seaplanes lay alongside it at the foot
of a steep wooden ramp. Behind the floating dock
was a large stationary one, set on tall wooden pilings.

"Wow!" Joe remarked. "The tide here must
rise to about twenty feet. It's at ebb now."

"Right. And at flood tide these docks must come
about level."

Walking briskly, the brothers descended the
ramp and talked with a mechanic servicing one of
the seaplanes.

"Is a fellow named Ted Sewell around?" Frank
asked. He was told that Ted had been there the
day before, but so far that day had not shown up.

"We'll come back later," Frank told the mechanic.

The brothers walked along the waterfront,
where rows of fishing boats thrust up a forest of
masts.

"I guess that people in Alaska either sail or fly,"
Joe said.

"With no roads to speak of, they have to,"
Frank pointed out. "You can't very well drive a
car into the bush."

The boys made several more inquiries about
Ted Sewell, but he had not been seen that day.
They also asked a dock guard about renting a

motorboat to take them to Tony's camp on the
Kooniak River.

"Sure, you can rent one easily," the watchman
told them. "But you'll have to wait till morning
and talk to the owners."

After walking up a steep hill the Hardys found
themselves in front of the Alaska Historical Museum, which was open that evening. They went
inside and studied the exhibits. Besides mounted
birds and animals, there were Indian and Eskimo
jewelry and wood carvings, bright-colored blankets, and baskets woven of fine rye grass.

"Look at this!" Joe said, pointing to a paper
enclosed under glass. It was a photostat of the
United States Treasury check to Russia for $7,-
200,000 for the purchase of Alaska.

"And think of all the gold that has been mined
here since then," Frank remarked. "Some bargain!"

They left the museum and wandered about the
city for a while, then returned to the dock.

"Eight o'clock and the sun is still high," Joe
marveled.

"We're almost in the land of the midnight sun,"
Frank said. "The clerk told me the sun won't set
until eleven P.M."

The air was quite cool and held a faint aroma
of fresh-caught fish mingled with the tang of
mountain pines. As they stood on the dock, a
motorboat came put-putting toward them. Its

lone occupant was a grizzled old man. His face was heavily whiskered and he wore a sea captain's cap.

"You fellers lookin' for a boat to rent?" he shouted up to them.

Frank nodded. "That's right. How did you know?"

"Watchman told me," the old man explained. "I'll hire this 'un out cheap. Come on down an' look it over. I'll even take you out for a spin."

The Hardys agreed eagerly and climbed down the nearest ladder to a pile of rocks near the water line. As they were about to board the boat, two shadowy figures loomed out from under the dock, grabbed the boys, and pinioned their arms in a viselike grip.

"A trap!" Joe shouted. *"Help!"*

His outcry was silenced by a blow on the head. Both boys were knocked unconscious.

CHAPTER III

Waterfront Search

FRANK was the first to revive. His feet were numb with cold, and he was biting on a thick wad of cloth. When he tried to move, his muscles ached painfully.

As his mind cleared, Frank realized he was bound and gagged. Then he remembered the grizzled old boatman and the sudden assault. His attackers had roped him to one of the wharf pilings!

A few feet away Joe was gagged and tied to another dock timber. He moaned as consciousness returned.

Suddenly Frank realized their feet were dangling in the icy water. Already the waves were lapping above their ankles. The tide was rising, and the slimy dock pilings showed the high-water mark was more than a foot above their heads!

Frantically the two boys scanned the harbor.

The only movement in sight was the sail of a fishing boat far out beyond the breakwater. Who would notice their plight in the semidarkness under the dock?

Some time later, back at the hotel, Chet awoke, from his nap. With a mighty yawn, the stout boy heaved himself out of bed.

"Getting dark out," he noticed, switching on the bedside lamp and glancing at his wrist watch. "Wow! Five after eleven! Wonder if Frank and Joe are back yet?"

Chet opened the connecting door and peered into the Hardys' room. Their beds were empty.

Alarmed, Chet hurried down to the lobby and inquired at the desk. After checking the key rack, the hotel clerk assured him that the Hardys had not returned.

"Now what do I do?" Chet wondered desperately. After a moment's thought he decided that the most likely place to pick up their trail seemed to be the waterfront. Perhaps they had met Ted Sewell there.

Striding along quickly, Chet made his way to the docks and paced along the seaplane base and rows of fishing boats.

"Frank! Joe!" he called. There was no answer.

Then Chet noticed a watchman lounging against a shed, smoking his pipe.

"Have you seen two young fellows around here?" Chet asked.

The watchman frowned and scratched his jaw. "Oh sure! I remember now. There was two lads here a couple o' hours ago. Asked me about rentin' a boat."

"Any idea where they went?"

The watchman gestured with his pipe. "They strolled out there on the dock. That's the last I seen of 'em."

Chet walked out on the dock to scan the harbor. Perhaps, he thought hopefully, his companions had hired a boat and gone out for a spin. But there was no craft in sight on the darkening waters.

As Chet stood wondering what to do next, he heard a muffled noise. *Bump! . . . Bump!*

The sound seemed to come from under the dock. Getting down on his hands and knees, Chet peered over the side of the dock, but he could make out nothing in the heavy gloom.

"Frank! . . . Joe!" he called again.

In response came a series of frantic whimpering noises. The eerie sounds sent a chill down Chet's spine! He jumped to his feet and ran back to the watchman's shed. "Someone's trapped under the dock!" he cried out.

"You must be imaginin' things, sonny."

"Oh, no, I'm not!" Chet insisted. After a brief

argument, he talked the watchman into launching a small dory. Still grumbling, the man rowed out along the pier while Chet aimed a flashlight among the wooden pilings.

Presently Chet gasped, "Frank! Joe! There they are!" By now, the water was up to the boys' chests.

The watchman's eyes popped. "Great jumpin' Jehoshaphat!" he cried.

After jockeying the boat into position, the watchman whipped out his jackknife and went to work on the ropes. Chet helped him. Finally they freed the two youths and hauled them aboard.

Both Frank and Joe were numb with cold. Their teeth were chattering so hard that at first neither could speak.

The watchman rowed ashore quickly and hustled the brothers into his shed, where Chet wrapped them in blankets. The watchman heated some milk on his potbellied stove. As Frank and Joe gulped the nourishing liquid, their strength slowly returned.

"What happened?" Chet asked, when they were able to talk.

Frank told how the whiskered old boatman had lured them into an ambush. "I didn't get much of a look at the men who grabbed us, but I'd say they were slender and about medium height."

"Right," Joe added. "That's all I could make out, too. Their faces were masked."

"That old feller was lyin'," the watchman declared. "No one asked me if you two lads were lookin' fer a boat to rent."

"He may have trailed us and overheard our conversation," Frank said. "Or maybe it was just a shrewd guess."

If the man *had* been guessing about their need for a boat, Joe reflected, this might mean he knew the Hardys were going to the Kooniak River.

"Want me to call the police?" the watchman asked sympathetically.

The young sleuths exchanged glances, then shook their heads. "We'll let it go till morning," Frank replied. "The police probably couldn't do much tonight, anyhow, and we both need a good rest."

Early the next morning the boys breakfasted at the hotel, then went to Juneau Police Headquarters. The sergeant who took their report was a former Seattle policeman, who knew Fenton Hardy by reputation.

"I'll send a man down to the docks with you," he said. "Maybe he can help you spot that boatman."

A short, heavy-set detective, named Phil Grant, made a tour of the boat dock and seaplane base with the three boys. Grant, who was well acquainted around the waterfront, asked numerous people if they knew anyone who fitted the Hardys' description of the boatman. No one recalled such a person.

"Looks as if we're up against a blank wall," the detective remarked as they halted on the wharf.

"I'm beginning to think those whiskers and the cap were just a disguise," Frank commented.

"Same here," Joe agreed. "In fact we can't even be sure he was an *old* man. He might have been wearing a gray wig."

Detective Grant shook his head doubtfully. "If so, we haven't much to go on, but we'll keep working on the case. I'll let you know if we turn up any clues."

"Thanks. We'll do the same," Frank told him.

Chet looked around nervously after the detective walked away. "Do you suppose those crooks are still trailing us?" he asked.

"Don't get jumpy." Joe chuckled. "I doubt if they'd try anything in broad daylight. Seriously, Frank, what do you think their game is?"

His brother shrugged. "Too early to answer that question yet. We'll know more after we've talked to Tony. But I'd say those guys who attacked us are part of a well-organized gang trying to scare us off this case."

Chet shuddered. "W-w-well, they're doing a good job so far as I'm concerned."

"For a guy who's scared you're doing a great detective job, Chet," Frank remarked.

"You saved our lives," Joe reminded the stocky youth.

The gratitude and praise gave Chet courage.

"Okay, fellows," he said. "Let's find Ted Sewell this time."

Again the three boys strolled out on the dock, inhaling gusts of the briny northern air. The harbor was bustling with activity as the fishing boats put out for the day's work. Shouts echoed across the water as the skippers barked orders to their crews.

Joe pointed to a motorboat slicing straight toward them. At the wheel was a husky blond youth about sixteen years old. "I wonder if that's the fellow we're looking for?"

Frank called to him as he drew alongside the dock. "Are you Ted Sewell?"

"That's right," the boy replied. "You fellows must be Frank and Joe Hardy and Chet Morton. Tony sent me to get you."

The three boys watched as the blond youth made his boat fast and scrambled up the ladder. They liked his friendly, open face.

"Sorry I didn't meet you yesterday," Ted apologized. "Motor trouble." As he spoke, the young skipper pulled a note from his pocket and handed it to Frank. It was in Tony Prito's handwriting and read:

Dear Frank and Joe:
This will introduce my friend, Ted Sewell.
He's a swell guy and you can trust him completely. Please come out to my camp on the

*Kooniak River as soon as you can. Be seeing
you soon, I hope.*

Regards,
Tony

"Okay," said Frank, folding up the letter.
"How soon can we leave?"

"Soon as you fellows are ready," Ted replied.

"We'll need some camping gear," Joe pointed
out.

"Maybe Ted can come along and show us a
place to buy our outfits."

"Sure. Be glad to."

"How about grub?" Chet put in anxiously.
"Will Tony have enough for all of us?"

Noting Chet's rotund physique, Ted grinned.
"Don't worry! You'll eat fine!"

An hour later, after loading their new pup tent
and sleeping bags into the boat, the boys shoved
off from Juneau. Ted steered down the Gastineau
Channel between mountainous Douglas Island
and the mainland, then southeastward along the
coast. A tangy scent of spruce and cedar drifted
down from the steep slopes.

"Nice boat you've got here," Frank remarked.
Although it had obviously seen hard use, the craft
looked powerful and seaworthy.

"It's part of Tony's outfit," the boy explained. "I've just been using it these past few

mornings to come to Juneau. Most of the time I scoot around in a little outboard."

"Doing what?" Joe asked.

"Beachcombing." The youth grinned. "I cruise around the beaches looking for old propellers, boat fittings, or scrap metal. Doesn't sound like much, but I earn quite a bit selling the stuff."

"Sounds like a great outdoor life," Frank said. "How's Tony getting along?"

The boy's face clouded. "He likes his work fine, but he's plenty worried. He's been having trouble on his job and— Well, you'd better wait and get the whole story from Tony. I hear he sent for you fellows because you're good at solving mysteries."

"We've worked on quite a few cases," Frank admitted.

"Then I wish you'd solve a mystery for *me*," Ted said wistfully. "My father has disappeared."

CHAPTER IV

Cheechako Trouble

IMMEDIATELY it occurred to Frank that Mr. Sewell's disappearance might have some connection with Tony's trouble. He decided not to mention it, however, until he learned more about the mystery.

"Tell us what happened, Ted," Frank said sympathetically.

"Dad was working for the Fish and Wildlife Service, same as Tony," the boy explained. "About two weeks ago he left Juneau on a survey trip into the wilderness to check on upstream feeding conditions for the salmon. He was due back in five or six days but never returned."

"Was a search made?" Chet asked.

"Sure. The Service sent out a helicopter, also a ground party with an Indian guide, but they couldn't find the slightest trace of him."

Ted bit his lip and tried to keep his voice from

breaking. "They're afraid Dad may have been mauled by a bear or—or met with some other accident."

"We're sorry, Ted," Joe murmured gravely.

"Maybe," Frank added, "we can turn up a clue to your dad while we're helping Tony."

"Thanks, fellows."

The companions cruised along in silence for a while, past thick, mysterious forests of evergreen. The offshore waters were dotted with islands and the rugged coast line was notched by inlets and streams pouring out of the wilderness.

"These must be pretty tricky waters for a ship to navigate," Joe remarked.

Ted Sewell nodded. "There've been a lot of wrecks along the Inside Passage to Alaska. I'll show you one of them."

As they passed Admiralty Island, Ted pointed out a rotting, salt-bleached hulk sticking out of the water. "That was a schooner named the *Islander*," he told the boys. "It was wrecked years ago while carrying Klondike gold miners back to the States."

"What happened to the passengers?" Frank asked.

"They jumped overboard. Most of them were so weighted down with their pokes of gold that they sank right to the bottom."

Chet shuddered. "Boy, I hope their ghosts don't haunt this neck of the woods!"

Friendly banter continued until almost noon, when they reached the mouth of the Kooniak River. Flanked by dense timber on both banks, its ice-cold waters flowed clear as crystal.

"The Kooniak runs from the northeast," Ted told his companions. "The headwaters are some-where up in Canada." He turned the boat into the river and steered toward a small island about a quarter of a mile upstream. Ahead, the boys could see a plume of smoke rising from a camp-fire near a sturdy tent.

As they drew closer, a dark-haired lad rushed out and ran to the shore. He wore a T-shirt, dungarees, and leather jacket.

"There's Tony!" Joe shouted.

"Hi, fellows!" Tony called, waving his arms.

"I'm glad that he's all right," Frank said quietly as the trio waved back.

Ted brought the boat up to a small wooden dock which extended a few yards out into the water. One by one, the boys clambered out to shake hands happily with Tony.

"Welcome to Alaska!" Tony said, chuckling. "The forty-ninth state! Twice as big as Texas and—"

"Ten times as dangerous!" Chet cut in.

"It won't be for long," Tony went on. "Not with you fellows here to figure things out!"

"What's been going on?" Frank asked.

"Tell you about it later. Let's eat first. I figured

Ted would be back about this time, so lunch is on the fire."

"Mm, that's for me!" Chet crooned, sniffing the appetizing aroma of pork and beans.

Ted offered to set the rustic pine table while Tony showed his friends around the camp.

"Not that there's much to show," Tony added. "You can walk around this whole island in half an hour."

The young stream guard led the way toward the upper end of the island. Aside from a few clumps of trees and underbrush, it was barren of cover, permitting a good view in all directions.

"That's one reason I'm stationed here, rather than on shore," Tony explained. "This location enables me to keep a better lookout for poachers who might try entering the river."

"What's the other reason?" Joe asked.

"Bears. There are quite a few of them over on the mainland, but they never bother me here."

"Then I'm staying put on this island!" Chet declared firmly.

"Funny name, the Kooniak River," Frank mused. "What does it mean?"

"Search me," Tony replied. "It's an Indian name, I guess, but I haven't learned their lingo yet—except *cheechako*."

"What's that?" Joe inquired.

"What you fellows are." Tony chuckled. "New-comers, or tenderfeet. That's what the old-time sourdoughs used to call all the greenhorns who came up here during the gold rush."

By this time, they had reached a point facing directly upstream. Here the river formed a sparkling six-foot waterfall. The swift-flowing stream filled the air with spray as it plunged over the rocks.

"The salmon jump those falls on their way upstream to spawn," Tony said with a gesture. "I'll show you tonight."

"Why wait?" Joe put in eagerly. "Can't we see 'em now?"

Tony shook his head. "When humans are around, the salmon travel upstream after dark."

Returning to camp, the boys found the meal ready. Ted ladled out platefuls of beans, and everyone ate with a keen appetite. After a dessert of canned fruit and cookies, the boys leaned back with sighs of satisfaction.

"Now, Tony," Joe said, "give us the story of the goings-on here."

"Okay. The trouble started right after I arrived," Tony began. "A fishing boat put in at the mouth of the river, and the crew tried to bribe me to leave my post."

"Then what?" Chet asked, wide-eyed.

"I told 'em to scram," Tony said disgustedly. "If I'd left this spot unguarded, those crooks would have seined all the fish out of the river. And it's my job to see that they don't! This is protected water."

"Did you report the incident?" Frank inquired.

"Sure," Tony nodded. "I sent word to the authorities in Juneau and a couple of special agents came here. They staked out undercover and kept watch for three days, but nothing happened. Then, the very night after they left, someone took some pot shots at me while I was sleeping. You can see the bullet holes in my tent." He pointed to rents in the khaki covering.

"Wow!" Chet exclaimed. "You must be up against a dangerous bunch!"

"You're telling me!" said Tony. "Seems to me that ordinary fish poachers wouldn't risk a murder. The way I figured, something big must be going on and someone's awfully anxious to get me away from here. That's when I decided to send for you fellows."

Frank and Joe mulled over this information while Ted prepared to leave in his own small outboard motorboat. The others accompanied him down to the dock and unloaded the pup tent and sleeping bags from Tony's boat.

Ted shook hands all around before shoving off. "Nice meeting you fellows," he said earnestly. "If you get a chance, I hope you can solve the mystery of my father's disappearance."

"We'll try," Frank promised.

Later, after the pup tent had been erected and the sleeping bags stowed, the Hardys told Tony about their own adventures since receiving his telegram.

"I think you're right, Tony," Joe concluded. "There's a gang behind all this, and they're after something bigger than salmon. If that spy Stransky is mixed up in it, they may be a foreign group."

Frank's eyes narrowed and he snapped his fingers. "You know, Aunt Gertrude may have given us a valuable clue!"

"What do you mean?" Joe asked.

"That moon rocket she told us about. If it dropped in this area, foreign agents may be trying to find it before any Americans do."

"That makes sense," Joe agreed. "Maybe we've got a rocket search on our hands after all."

The afternoon passed quickly while the boys busied themselves with camp chores. At seven o'clock they ate supper, then talked over their plans until nightfall. When it was dark, Tony said, "Come on. I'll show you a real salmon run!"

The boys crossed to the west bank by boat, then made their way along the shore to the falls. The moon had gone behind a cloud, so Tony aimed his flashlight toward the cascading waters. The others gasped at the spectacle.

"Oh, man! What I'd give to cast a line in there!" Chet exclaimed.

The river was alive with salmon! Glinting pink and silver in the beam of light, the fish were leaping and wriggling their way up the six-foot falls.

"Talk about a subway rush!" Joe chuckled. "What makes them so anxious to get upriver?"

"Sort of a homing instinct," Tony replied. "When they're two to six years old, depending on the species, they head back to fresh water where they were born. Then they lay their eggs and die."

To keep from frightening the salmon, Tony used his light only in brief flashes. One of the flashes revealed a set of stone steps in the waterfall.

"It's called a ladder," Tony explained. "The Fish and Wildlife Service installs them in many streams to help the salmon make their leaps."

By the time they returned to camp, the newcomers were yawning and ready to crawl into their sleeping bags. The next morning, after a refreshing sleep, they ate a hearty breakfast of bacon, eggs, and fried potatoes. Then Frank suggested that they make a tour of the island to check for clues.

"Good idea," Tony agreed.

As they strode along, the Hardys kept constantly on the alert for any signs of a sneak visit by their enemies. Suddenly Joe let out a cry.

"Look!" he exclaimed, pointing to the ground ahead.

A fresh trail of footprints led from the under-brush down to the water and back! They had obviously been made by two persons. Frank studied the prints with keen interest and called his brother's attention to the heelmarks. Each contained a circle and star.

"The same kind of heelmarks Stransky made back at the Bayport airfield," Frank commented.

"Good night! You don't mean that same guy is *here* too?" Chet burst out.

Frank shook his head. "Stransky couldn't have made both sets of prints, even if he managed to break jail. But they may have been made by men working with him or for him."

"The same guys who took those pot shots at me?" Tony asked with a worried look.

Frank shrugged. "No telling, but these prints aren't more than a few hours old. Whoever made them was here on the island last night!"

CHAPTER V

A Strange Knapsack

A SILENCE fell on the campers as the full import of Frank's words sank home.

"What I'd like to know," Joe put in, "is how those prowlers got here. If that same fishing boat came back during the night, we'd have heard it."

"I doubt if they'd have taken a chance on waking us," Frank said thoughtfully. "Seems more likely they came in a canoe."

Joe spoke up. "You could be right about that, Frank. They might even have come from somewhere upriver and portaged around the falls."

Frank nodded. "I think we should scout this whole area from the air. That would give us a chance to learn the terrain and all the streams around here."

"Swell idea!" Joe agreed. "We might even spot the enemy camp!"

Tony, whose equipment included a two-way radio, volunteered to call the Fish and Wildlife

Service in Juneau. "They put a helicopter into service just a few months ago," he informed the others. "I'm sure that we could arrange a flight."

"Good! How about calling them right now?" Frank urged.

Tony did so, and the official on duty promised to send the helicopter to the island early the next morning.

That afternoon, while Tony attended to writing out some reports and Chet stretched out for a nap, Frank and Joe decided to explore the riverbank above the falls.

The two boys crossed over from the island by motorboat, then hiked northward along the rising shore line. The ground underfoot was soft with a thick layer of pine needles and mossy vegetation.

"Feels like walking on a carpet," Joe remarked.

"Just right for moccasins," said Frank. "But I could sure do without the mosquitoes!"

When they were several hundred yards past the falls, Frank pointed through the trees to an object in the river. "Take a look at that rock out there, Joe. Pretty unusual, eh?"

Joe shaded his eyes and squinted at the curious pillar of stone. Rising almost six feet above the water, it was black and shaped like an hourglass. The spray from the rapids made it glisten in the sunshine.

"It sure *is* odd!" Joe agreed. "I wonder if it's a natural formation?"

"Let's find out," Frank proposed.

The brothers pushed through a thick grove of brush and alders which grew almost to the river's edge. Here the Hardys removed their shoes and socks, rolled up their pants, and waded out into the stream.

"Wow! This water's ice cold!" Joe exclaimed.

"Watch out for those sharp stones on the bottom," Frank said.

The black rock stood only a few yards from shore. It was smooth and weathered, showing no signs of having been chipped or chiseled into shape by tools.

"Funny how it narrows in the middle," Frank said. "Could the water alone have done that?"

"Probably," Joe mused, "it gets worn away by silt and debris when the river's—"

The words ended in a yell of surprise as Joe was suddenly knocked flat by a huge paw. With a splash, he landed in the water! Frank, whirling, saw an enormous brown bear! A menacing growl rumbled from its jaws.

Before the bear could aim another blow, Frank plunged into the icy rapids. Balked, the huge beast then turned back to his first target. Joe was stunned and floundering in the shallow water. The bear's claws arced toward him in a vicious swipe! But Frank yanked his brother's arm, pulling him out of the way. The bear's paw missed Joe by inches!

Towing Joe with one hand, Frank swam frantically out of range. The foaming rapids threatened to sweep them toward the falls, but fortunately, the two boys were strong swimmers and finally reached the shore.

Meanwhile the bear, towering erect on his hind legs, glared at the youths with hot, suspicious eyes. Luckily he made no move to pursue them.

"What a monster!" Joe gasped, as the Hardys sank down on the bank. "He must be nine feet tall!"

"At least," Frank panted. "And I'll bet he weighs close to a ton!"

Joe shivered in his soaked clothing. "What made him so mad? I thought those fellows seldom attacked humans unless they're provoked."

"There's your answer." Frank chuckled wryly. "We *did* provoke him—by trespassing on his private fishing spot!"

Down on all fours again, the bear had just speared a plump salmon with one stroke of his paw. Flopping back on his haunches in the water, the huge animal devoured the fish in a few gulps. *Splat!* Another salmon fell prey to his mighty paw. This too disappeared down his gullet, followed by half a dozen others in quick succession. At last, his hunger satisfied, the bear lumbered out of the water and vanished among the alders.

"Whew!" Joe let out a whistle of relief. "I'm sure not sorry to see that baby leave!"

A menacing growl rumbled from the bear's jaws

"That makes two of us," Frank murmured. "Let's get back to camp before we freeze in these wet clothes!"

Dripping and shivering, the Hardys trudged back along the riverbank.

"Hold it!" Joe exclaimed, stopping suddenly. He bent down and plucked a battered knapsack out of the underbrush. "I wonder who lost this?"

"Take a look inside," Frank suggested. "Maybe there'll be some clue to the owner."

Joe unbuckled the straps and groped inside the pouch. "No. It's empty," he announced, holding the bag open for Frank to see.

"Wait a minute! I think there's an extra thickness of leather in there." Frank took the knapsack and ran his fingers around the interior. "Sure enough! There's a secret pocket!"

Joe's eyes gleamed with interest as Frank removed the contents. There were two items. One was a piece of jade, carved in the likeness of a fierce-looking bird. The other was a crumpled piece of paper.

"A map!" Frank exclaimed, unfolding the paper.

"Of what?" Joe stared in puzzlement. The map, crudely drawn, showed a river or stream of water and various other geographical features. But it bore no place names.

"Maybe Tony will recognize it," Frank said. "Come on! Let's hurry!"

Chet and Tony greeted the two bedraggled figures in astonishment. When the Hardys related their close call with the bear, Chet grew visibly pale. The brothers next displayed the knapsack and contents. Then, while Frank and Joe changed into dry clothes, Tony produced a map of the area from among his gear.

"This sketch doesn't jibe with any of the places on my map," he reported.

"This jade carving doesn't add up, either," Joe said thoughtfully. "Matter of fact, I've never heard of jade being found in Alaska. Have you?" he added, turning to his brother with a questioning look.

Frank shook his head. "It certainly doesn't look like any of the Indian carvings we saw in the museum."

Chet regarded the objects nervously. "If you ask me, this knapsack was left there as a t-t-trap," he quavered. "You fellows shouldn't have brought it back to camp. I'll bet this means another visit from our enemies!"

"How long do you suppose the knapsack had been lying there?" Tony asked, half inclined to agree with Chet.

"Not too long," Frank replied. "The buckles aren't even rusty."

Chet hastily looked around. "What'd I tell you? I'll bet someone's spying on us right now!"

CHAPTER VI

Nightmare!

THEY crouched quickly and glanced about. Then Frank broke into a grin. "Cut it out, Chet. Quit scaring me like that!"

"Just the same," Joe declared seriously, "there might be something to what Chet says. I think we'd better radio to Juneau about that knapsack." Tony cranked up the aerial of his radio. When the set was warmed up, he spoke into the microphone: "Kooniak calling Fish and Wildlife Service!"

Presently a voice crackled: "Juneau to Kooniak! Come in, please!"

Tony reported the finding of the knapsack. The department operator promised to inform the police by telephone and then to call back.

In a few minutes the operator's voice came over the speaker. "The police say that no such loss has been reported. But our man will pick up the knapsack for them when he flies out with the helicopter."

"Okay, thanks," Tony said. "Over and out."

After a hearty supper, the boys washed up their mess kits and talked for a while around the campfire. When they were ready to retire, Chet seemed nervous.

"I still think we may get a return visit from that gang," Chet insisted. "How about taking turns standing watch tonight?"

"Okay. That's not a bad idea," Frank said. "Let's draw straws to pick our watches."

Joe won and chose to stand the first trick. Chet, Frank, and Tony would follow in that order. It was broad daylight through most of Joe's watch. Finally, yawning, he woke Chet and prepared to crawl into his own sleeping bag.

As the plump youth took over, the birdcalls became hushed. The sky flamed red, then a deep, brooding twilight settled over the pine forest.

"These woods are positively spooky at night!" Chet thought with a shiver. Picking himself a comfortable spot, he sat down under a tree. "No use getting nervous. I'd better think of something cheerful!"

Determinedly Chet concentrated on visions of himself salmon fishing—pulling in one silvery fish after another. This did make him feel better.

Night deepened. Soon it was completely dark, except for the circle of light around the campfire. From across the river came the melancholy hoot of an owl.

Chet, lulled by the peacefulness of the night, settled himself more comfortably against the tree. "This isn't such a bad spot after all," he thought drowsily. The next instant Chet sat bolt upright and a horrified yell escaped his lips. The Hardys and Tony awoke in a flash and came rushing out of their tents.

"Chet! What's wrong?" Frank cried out.

The chunky lad was on his feet, trembling. "S-s-something came at me out of the darkness!" he quavered.

"You mean an animal?" Tony asked.

"No—men! A whole gang of them! They tried to club me, but I fought 'em off!"

"*What?*" Tony stared at him. "You must be dreaming! There's no one around here but us!"

"But I saw them, I tell you!" Chet insisted, still shaking with fright. "Masked men!"

Frank and Joe quickly scouted the ground around the camp. But there were no footprints or other traces of intruders.

"Exactly where did all this happen?" Frank inquired calmly.

"Right here," Chet replied. "I was sitting with my back against this tree, and all of a sudden—"

"—you fell asleep!" Joe completed the sentence with a chuckle. "You just had a nightmare!"

To reassure their friend, the Hardys and Tony took lanterns and made a thorough search. Finally Chet agreed that he must have dreamed the whole incident.

"Go ahead and hit the sack," Frank told him with a grin. "It's almost time for my watch, anyhow."

At breakfast the next morning Joe and Tony ribbed the stocky youth about his wild dream. Chet took their jokes good-naturedly, adding, "At least these flapjacks are real. Slip me a few more, Frank!"

Breakfast over, they busied themselves with their morning chores. Soon after they finished washing up, the helicopter arrived from Juneau.

"I'm Robbie Robbins," the pilot introduced himself. He was a pleasant young man, sandy-haired, about twenty-two years old.

The boys shook hands and explained why they had sent for him. Then Frank showed the pilot the crude map which the Hardys had found in the knapsack. "Ever seen a place like this?"

Robbins studied the map and shook his head. "Not that I recall. But there are so many lakes and streams around here that I wouldn't want to say for sure. We'll keep our eyes open."

The helicopter had seats for three besides the pilot, but Chet elected to stay on the island with Tony. "You fellows do the exploring," he told Frank and Joe. "I feel safer on the ground!"

Robbie and the Hardys climbed aboard, and the helicopter took off. Soon the Kooniak appeared as a ribbon of blue winding among the evergreens. The pilot headed northward, working back and forth in widening sweeps across both sides of the river.

"I don't see any place that looks like this map," Joe remarked.

"No sign of a camp, either," Frank added, as he scanned the terrain with binoculars.

Several hours later the boys noticed a cluster of huts about a mile west of the Kooniak. "It's a Haida village," Robbie told the Hardys. "They're one of the Alaskan Indian tribes."

"Could we land and question them?" Frank inquired. "I'd like to find out if they've seen any strangers recently."

"Okay. But you may not find them very talkative," Robbie warned.

The helicopter descended slowly to the village clearing. Instead of running to meet their visitors, the Indians gathered to watch from a distance. Their dark, slanted eyes, set in coppery faces, stared impassively at the newcomers.

"They don't look very friendly," Joe muttered.

"Do they speak English?" Frank asked the pilot.

"Most of them do, although they may not admit it. Often they use the Chinook trading jargon in talking to strangers."

Seeing that the Indians made no move, the

pilot stepped forward. *"Klahowya!"* he said in a loud voice. Several men of the village returned his greeting.

"We're looking for some white men," Frank told them. "Have you seen any strangers around here?"

The Indians merely shrugged and shook their heads. "Looks as though we're not going to get much out of them," Robbie murmured.

"Let's circulate around the village," Frank suggested. "Maybe they'll open up a bit after they get used to us."

Robbins agreed, so the trio strolled around, peering at the Indian dwellings. Though crude, the houses were stoutly built and well chinked. Near each one stood wooden racks, with strings of fish drying in the sun.

Frank and Joe were intrigued by a number of small log structures, poised on stilts as high as a man's head. There was one beside each house, with a ladder going up to the entrance.

"What are those things?" Joe puzzled. "Oversized birdhouses?"

Robbie Robbins grinned. "No, they're caches," he explained, "for storing food out of reach of wild animals."

Several Indian children trailed around behind the white visitors, watching them curiously. Finally one teen-age boy grew bold enough to speak.

"Me Fleetfoot," he said to Frank.

"Glad to know you." Frank offered his hand, hoping to make friends with the boy. "I'm Frank Hardy. This is my brother Joe, and this is Robbie Robbins."

After pumping each one by the hand, the Indian youth continued, "You ask about strangers?"

"That's right," Frank said. "Have you seen any recently?"

"Nowitka! Yes," Fleetfoot replied. "One day I go to river to fish. See two white men drift downstream in big canoe. They make much talk."

"Did you hear what they were saying?" Joe asked eagerly.

The Haida lad paused, furrowing his brow as if trying to remember the exact words. "I hear one man say, 'They protect the salmon. The salmon protect us.' Then other man say something in strange lingo—not like American talk. Me not understand."

Joe shot an excited glance at his brother, who said, "Fleetfoot, will you do something for us?"

"Maybe." The Indian boy smiled and shrugged. "What do you want?"

"Next time you see those men, or any other strangers, trail them to their camp—but keep out of sight, so they don't see you. Then come and tell us. We'll be staying on the island at the mouth of the river."

The Indian boy looked uncertain.

"Maybe we can do something for you. What would you like?" Frank asked.

A broad grin spread over the young Indian's face. "Me like ride in big funny bird!"

"Our whirlybird." Robbie Robbins chuckled. "Okay, it's a deal, Fleetfoot."

Well satisfied with the results of their visit to the Indian village, Robbie and the Hardys took off again in the helicopter.

"Frank, it looks as though our guess was right," Joe said excitedly. "If one of those men spoke a strange language, we must be up against foreign agents!"

"It sounds that way," Frank agreed. "But I sure wish we knew what they're after. Let's hope Fleetfoot delivers on his end of the bargain!"

Continuing northward, the helicopter soared above the rolling foothills of the Alaskan coastal range. Beyond the timber line, the rocky slopes towered up to snow-capped peaks. One of the mountains drew Frank's attention by its strange contours.

"Gosh, look at that," he remarked, pointing out the unique formation to Joe. "Those peaks stick up just like four fingers and a thumb."

"A good description," Robbie put in. "The Indians call it Devil's Paw, and you can see why." He added, "That whole range up ahead forms the international boundary between Alaska and

British Columbia. Guess we'd better turn back."

On the return trip, Robbie circled over an enormous tongue of ice, seventeen miles long. Glittering blue-white in the sunshine, it trailed down from the mountain snow fields almost to the coast.

"Mendenhall Glacier," the pilot told Frank and Joe. "It's actually a river of ice."

The boys gaped at the spectacle. "A river?" Joe echoed. "You mean it flows?"

"Yes, but so slowly you could never tell by the naked eye," Robbie replied. "I guess *creeps* might be a better word."

Suddenly Frank exclaimed, "Go lower, Robbie! I think there are two people down there!"

The helicopter swooped toward the glacier. "You're right!" Joe cried. "A man and a woman! They must be stranded!" The tiny figures signaled frantically, waving their arms. They appeared to be seated on the ice.

"Can we rescue them?" Frank asked the pilot.

"We'll sure try!" Hovering into position above the two people, Robbie told the boys to unreel a rope ladder which he carried in the rear of the helicopter's cabin.

At sight of the ladder the man on the glacier shook his head and signaled with his arms.

"He wants someone to climb down and help them," Frank said. "I'll go!"

CHAPTER VII

Glacier Trek

THE helicopter hovered lower over the ice as
Frank prepared for the rescue. Easing himself out
of the cabin, he groped for a footing on one of the
metal rungs. The ladder swayed sickeningly as
he climbed down. But Frank kept a steady grasp.
Finally he reached the glacier. The middle-aged
couple, dressed in hiking garb, greeted him with
anxious relief.

"Sorry to put you to so much trouble. We're
certainly grateful that you responded to our signals!" The man, although he seemed to be in
pain, flashed a smile. "My wife and I had an accident. Our name's Turner. I'm an engineer."

Frank introduced himself, and Mrs. Turner,
a pleasant-faced woman, added her thanks.

"We had a nasty fall on the ice," she explained.
"I'm afraid my husband's leg is broken, and I
seemed to have sprained my arm quite badly.
Could you possibly take us aboard?"

"Of course, Mrs. Turner." Frank smiled re-
assuringly. After studying the situation, he removed two rungs of the ladder and improvised a
splint for Mr. Turner's leg. Then he lashed first
the woman, then the man, to the ladder and had
them lifted aboard.

"There won't be room for all of us," Joe told
the pilot. "Suppose I keep Frank company on
the glacier while you take Mr. and Mrs. Turner
to the hospital?"

"I guess that's the best plan," Robbie agreed.
He reached into a storage locker and took out
two pairs of steel cleats. "Here. You and Frank
fasten these to your shoes. They'll help you keep
your footing on the ice. I'll be back pronto to
pick you up."

"Okay, thanks." Joe pocketed the cleats, and
after wishing the Turners a speedy recovery from
their injuries, climbed down the ladder. Then
Robbie reeled it back aboard. The two boys
waved as the whirlybird took off toward Juneau.

"This is a chilly-looking spot, all right," Frank
remarked, gazing around at the vast expanse of
ice. "What a nasty place to have an accident!"

"You said it!" Joe replied. "Which reminds
me—we'd better put these on before we take a
spill ourselves!"

He handed Frank one set of cleats, and the
boys sat down on the ice to attach them to their
shoes. Feeling a bit more sure-footed, they de-

cided to do a little exploring while they waited for Robbie's return.

"Let's take a look farther up the gorge," Frank suggested.

"Suits me—if we can make it." Joe took a couple of trial steps, moving as gingerly as a man walking on eggs. "Boy, it's a good thing Robbie gave us these cleats, or I'd be flat on my back by now!"

Frank chuckled. "Keep your fingers crossed. It could still happen!"

In appearance, the glacier was more like a mountainous ridge than a river. Its surface was humped and uneven, as well as split with cracks and fissures. The boys made their way along slowly, enjoying the majestic view of the mountain slopes that rose on either side of the glacier.

Suddenly Frank let out a yell as he lost his footing. "Joe! Help!"

Joe threw himself flat on the ice and caught his brother by the arm in the nick of time. An instant later Frank would have slid into a yawning crevasse!

"Whew!" Frank lay panting for a moment after Joe had pulled him to safety. "That was too close for comfort! I didn't even notice that downslope till I hit the skids!"

"Maybe we'd better head for shore," Joe suggested. "This berg is too tricky to navigate."

"Second the motion!"

By the time they reached the timbered slope on the nearest side of the valley, a chill wind had sprung up. Blowing down from the mountains, it rustled the branches of the tall evergreens.

"I'm glad these fir trees act as a wind screen," Frank remarked with a shiver.

"Right now, I'd prefer the kind of furs we could wrap around us!" Joe retorted wryly.

Frank chuckled. "For making a pun like that, you *deserve* to freeze!"

As the moments of waiting dragged by, both boys began to feel hunger pangs from having missed lunch.

"Wow! Could I go for a square meal!" Joe groaned.

"Don't look now, but here comes someone with the same idea!" Frank pointed to a huge prowling bear which had just appeared among the underbrush, a hundred yards away.

"Oh—oh!" Joe turned pale. "I suddenly lost my appetite! Come on! We'd better go out on the ice!"

The Hardys hastily retraced their steps out over the glacier. After peering in their direction for a while with its nearsighted eyes and sniffing the air hungrily, the bear ambled off into the timber. The brothers heaved sighs of relief.

"Think it's safe to go back?" Joe asked.

"Let's not tempt him!" Frank cautioned.

"W-w-what's keeping Robbie?" Joe muttered,

his teeth chattering from the cold. More than an hour had passed.

"Search me," Frank replied. "It's not a long run into Juneau. Maybe he was delayed at the hospital."

Both boys were chilled to the bone and ravenously hungry when the drone of a plane's motor finally reached their ears. Shading their eyes against the dazzling sun glare, they saw a small single-engine craft wing into view. It flew in low above the treetops and circled overhead.

"The pilot's signaling to us!" Joe cried out.

The Hardys waved back.

"He's going to drop something," Frank said as they saw the cabin door open. The pilot shoved out a large package, and it plummeted to the ice a short distance away.

The boys rushed to examine it. "Let's hope it's food!" Joe exclaimed.

Frank cut the twine with his jackknife and tore off the heavy wrapping paper. Inside were a pair of sheepskin coats rolled around a cardboard box. The box, warm to the touch, proved to contain roast-beef sandwiches, two thermos bottles of cocoa, and a note from Robbie Robbins, which said:

> *Dear Frank and Joe:*
> *The copter is laid up for repairs, but here's something to keep you going. After you've*

*eaten, start walking toward the mouth of
the glacier. I'll send a car to meet you.*
                    Robbie Robbins

Frank read the note with a slight frown.
"Tough break," he commented.

"Never mind, let's eat!" said Joe cheerfully.
"My mouth's watering!"

The boys waved their thanks to the pilot, still
circling overhead. He dipped his wings in response and flew off. Frank and Joe donned the
sheepskins gratefully, then tackled the sandwiches with gusto. Their spirits rose with every
bite.

"Man, those tasted wonderful!" Joe said as he
swallowed the last mouthful. "Almost as good as
Mom's or Aunt Gertrude's!"

Frank agreed and finished his cocoa. "Let's get
going. We've got a long trip to the mouth of the
glacier."

Greatly invigorated, the Hardys began their
trek. At first they enjoyed the rugged grandeur
of the mountain scenery. They were snug in their
warm sheepskins, and the brisk wind blowing
down from the glacier made their blood tingle.

"When summer vacation started, I never
thought we'd wind up hiking on ice!" Joe remarked with a chuckle.

"We should have brought skates," Frank added
with a grin.

As the afternoon wore on, however, the boys began to feel the effects of the dangerous journey. Their leg muscles ached from the constant strain of keeping their footing on the ice.

"What say we try it over on the side of the valley again?" Frank suggested. "That bear's probably found himself another snack by now."

"We *hope!*" Joe quipped. "But okay. It can't be any worse than this."

Back on dry land, the boys found the going easier, in spite of the tumbled rocks and heavy underbrush. Nevertheless, the hours of steady trudging proved a grueling ordeal. By the time they reached the gravel road connecting with the Glacier Highway that led to Juneau, the Hardys were exhausted.

"Whew! What I'd give to be hitting the sack right now!" Joe groaned, sprawling full length on the ground.

"Let's hope we don't have to wait long for that car," Frank said, with a glance at his wrist watch. The time was eight minutes before 7:00 P.M.

By nine o'clock the car promised by Robbie had not arrived. "Joe, it'll be dark in two more hours," Frank said uneasily. "I think we should start walking toward town. Doesn't look as though that car is going to show up."

"Okay. But I'd sure like to know what's behind the delay!"

Wearily the boys set out. The sun went down and gradually dusk began to gather. A plane droned overhead, followed by a weird bird screech from the forest. Otherwise, the Alaskan wilderness seemed wrapped in silence. On and on the boys trudged, with the same harrowing thought in mind:

Had Robbie fallen victim to the Hardys' enemies, bent on preventing their rescue?

CHAPTER VIII

Salmon Raid

THOUGH becoming more tired and footsore every minute, Frank and Joe plodded on toward Juneau. Finally they reached the outskirts of the city, where the boys flagged a taxi.

"You fellows look bushed," the driver remarked as they climbed in. "Where to?"

"The seaplane base," Frank said.

Arriving at the dock, they questioned a guard about Robbie Robbins. He told the Hardys that both the pilot and his helicopter were gone. "Robbie took a passenger with him," the watchman reported. "Told me he was going to pick up two boys on Mendenhall Glacier."

The Hardys stared. "But we were told the copter was laid up for repairs!" Joe exclaimed. "A plane dropped us a note to that effect."

"Robbie did have some trouble with his steering rotor," the watchman conceded, "but that was five hours ago. Say, are you the two fellows he was talking about?"

"That's right." Frank declared. "The note said that he'd send a car for us, but it never showed up. Neither did the copter."

"How'd you get to Juneau?"

"We walked."

The dock guard shoved back his cap and scratched his forehead. "That's funny." A troubled frown spread over his weather-beaten face. "Hanged if I can figure it out! Didn't you sight his copter on the way?"

The boys shook their heads, and Joe asked, "Who was his passenger?"

"A man," the watchman replied, "but I didn't get much of a look at him, only from a distance. By thunder, I hope nothing's happened to Robbie! He may have had an accident!"

The Hardys were equally concerned, although they refrained from mentioning their fears of foul play. "Any chance of sending out a plane to look for him?" Frank asked.

"Sure! The bush pilots around here always keep a search plane on stand-by." Much perturbed, the watchman bustled into his booth and made a phone call to arrange for an immediate take-off.

Realizing there was nothing more they could do for the time being, the Hardys hurried to the Baranof Hotel and checked in for the night. Too tired even to think of food, the brothers tumbled into bed.

The next morning Frank and Joe returned to the seaplane dock. To their dismay, there was still no news of Robbie, nor had his helicopter been sighted.

"We'd better notify the police," Frank decided. "Then I vote we head back to the island."

At police headquarters Detective Grant jotted down the details of their story and promised to send out an alert to all authorities in the state. "We still have no lead on that gang who ambushed you fellows at the dock," he added. "But if Robbins has met with foul play, it may be the work of the same group."

After promising to keep in touch, the boys left headquarters, pausing outside to discuss their plans. "We'll have to get ourselves a motorboat," Joe decided.

"And a canoe, too," Frank suggested. They had little difficulty renting a powerful, trim-looking craft. The owner also provided a sturdy canoe, which they attached by a towline to the motorboat. The brothers embarked and headed down the Gastineau Channel. Eager to reach the island, Frank ran the boat at full power for most of the trip.

As they neared the mouth of the Kooniak,

the distant sound of gunfire reached their ears.

"Shots!" Joe exclaimed. "Tony and Chet must be in trouble!"

Frank nodded grimly. Jerking the throttle wide open, he sent the motorboat roaring ahead through the choppy water. Its bow leaped clear of the waves, showering the Hardys with spray.

As they rounded a point and turned into the river, another rifleshot cracked—then another! Frank and Joe stared in dismay. A man, in a small speedboat driven by a companion, was sniping at the occupants of the island. Tony and Chet had apparently dodged for cover among the trees. Meanwhile, three boatloads of fishermen were hauling in wriggling masses of salmon with huge nylon seines.

"Those crooks!" Joe gritted between clenched teeth. "They couldn't bribe Tony, so now they're using bullets to keep him out of action while they pull off their salmon raid!"

"Even those seines they're using are against the law!" Frank added. Suddenly he whipped the boat around in a fast turn. Joe, startled, exclaimed, "Hey, what's the idea?"

"We can't stop them singlehanded," his brother pointed out, "but maybe we can get help. I don't think they've spotted us yet."

"We can't go all the way back to Juneau," Joe objected. "There isn't time!"

"No, but I'm hoping this boat may be

equipped with a radio," Frank said. "Take a look in the rear locker!"

Joe did so and let out a jubilant yelp. "You're right! A two-way set! I'll warm 'er up!"

In a few moments he had the set sputtering and crackling. Not knowing the proper frequency for either the Juneau police or the Fish and Wildlife Service, Joe left the tuning untouched while he issued a few trial calls over the microphone. Almost immediately a ham operator responded.

"This is Luke Burton near Ketchikan," the voice said. "Come in, please."

Joe explained the situation, and Burton replied, "Poachers, eh? Just stand by and I'll raise Juneau in a hurry. They'll have the law down there so fast those guys won't know what hit 'em!"

The boys cruised out of sight beyond the point to await developments. Burton was as good as his word. Presently the drone of aircraft was heard, and two seaplanes came swooping down to a splash landing in the mouth of the river.

Joe gave an exuberant whoop. "Let's get in there and watch the fireworks!"

Grinning, Frank steered the boat back into the Kooniak. Armed enforcement agents were already covering the poachers with carbines and barking out orders through megaphones. Sullenly the fishermen emptied their seines, then brought their boats alongside the waiting planes.

The speedboat, hemmed in between the waterfall upstream and the patrol planes at the mouth of the river, was also forced to surrender. An agent went aboard each of the fishing craft, and the speedboat was taken in tow.

"Are you the fellows who radioed the alarm?" the officer in charge asked the Hardys as Frank maneuvered within speaking distance.

"We contacted a ham near Ketchikan," Joe explained through cupped hands. "He relayed word to Juneau!"

"Nice work!" the man called back. "Come on ashore and we'll see what these poachers have to say for themselves!"

As the Hardys approached the island, they were relieved to see Tony and Chet running to greet them.

"You fellows all right?" Frank asked, as he and Joe climbed out on the little wooden dock.

"Sure, thanks to you two!" Tony replied. "But things were getting mighty hot with those bullets kicking up dirt around us!"

"I thought it was curtains for us!" Chet gasped, still shaking with excitement.

"Why didn't you radio for help when those guys first showed up?" Joe asked.

"I tried to," Tony explained, "but another radio kept jamming my signal. I judge it was a powerful set and not far away. After that, the snipers started shooting at us and we headed for the trees. I didn't get another chance to send."

Meanwhile, the enforcement agents were herding the poachers ashore for questioning. There were nine in the group, including the two from the speedboat. Unshaven and rough-looking, in dungarees and wool jerseys, they faced their captors with sullen expressions.

The agent in charge, who knew of the previous attempt to fish the Kooniak, asked Tony, "Ever seen any of these men before?"

The stream guard studied them with an uncertain frown. "No, sorry, but I don't recognize any of them."

One hulking fellow, evidently the ringleader, spoke up, "You can't pin anything else on us! This the first time we ever fished around here!"

"Your last time too!" the agent snapped.

"What about those bullets that were fired at Tony's tent?" Frank put in. "Maybe we can make a ballistic comparison," he suggested to the chief agent, hoping that one of the group might be panicked into confessing.

But the sniper snorted scornfully, "Go ahead and compare! Them bullets won't fit *my* gun!"

The poachers also denied having any part in Robbie Robbins' disappearance, or in jamming Tony's transmitter. The latter claim seemed borne out by the fact that there was no radio equipment in any of their boats capable of jamming a broadcast signal.

After the prisoners and agents had left, the four

boys gathered around the campfire to talk over the events of the past two days.

"I'll make us some cocoa and hot dogs," Chet volunteered. "A fellow needs something to keep up his strength after an experience like that!"

"At least it hasn't affected your appetite," Joe teased. "Not that anything could!"

Tony reported that he and Chet had had no trouble up to the time the raiders appeared. Then Frank and Joe told about their visit to the Haida village, their adventure on the glacier, and their forced trek into Juneau. Their two companions listened with keen interest. Tony was especially intrigued to learn about the Indian boy's report of seeing two strange white men in a canoe.

"Those fellows *must* be mixed up with the gang," Tony remarked, "because they never showed themselves in the open around here."

"Maybe they didn't come this far down river," Chet put in.

"Where else would they be going?" Joe argued. "Frank and I didn't spot any camp between here and the Indian village. And we looked hard!"

"What puzzles me is that short-wave jamming," Frank mused. "Try your set now, Tony, and see if you get a clear signal."

Tony did so, and was able to contact Juneau without any difficulty. After the boys had finished their hot dogs and cocoa, they strolled toward the north end of the island.

"I'd sure like to know if those salmon poachers had anything to do with the jamming," Frank went on.

"They had no equipment," Joe reminded him.

Frank admitted this, but added, "It's too much of a coincidence that the jamming was timed just when they made their raid."

Conjecturing broke off suddenly as Tony yelled, "Look!" and pointed downstream.

A lone figure, standing upright in a canoe, was about to plunge over the falls!

CHAPTER IX

Fleetfoot's News

IN SECONDS the foaming rapids would sweep the canoeist to disaster!

"His boat'll be swamped!" Joe gasped. "Come on! Let's help him!"

Casting anxious glances over their shoulders, the boys raced back to the dock to launch their own canoe. But they halted in amazement as the other craft took the plunge over the falls like a graceful sea bird!

"Hold it!" Frank called out. "That fellow doesn't need help!"

"It's Fleetfoot!" Joe exclaimed.

Balancing himself with his paddle, the Indian lad shot through the spray and landed, still upright, at the foot of the falls. Then, with a few rapid strokes of his blade, he propelled himself toward the island.

"Whew!" Chet gulped, mopping beads of perspiration from his forehead. "That Indian must have wings!"

The boys hurried down to the shore to greet Fleetfoot, who was already beaching his canoe.

"You really gave us a scare, Fleetfoot," Frank told him.

"You mean when I shoot rapids?" The Indian boy grinned. "No scare! White water is fun! Sometime I teach you how."

In spite of the case with which he had shot the falls, Fleetfoot seemed to be bursting with inner excitement. "Me have message and have come for whirlybird ride!" he informed Frank proudly.

"I'm sorry, Fleetfoot," Frank explained. "You may have to wait for your ride. The copter is missing, and so is the man who makes it fly."

The Indian lad's face darkened with disappointment. "You mean—you break promise."

"Now hold on, Fleetfoot," Frank said gently. He put his hand on the boy's shoulder and looked him straight in the eye. "I'm speaking the truth. Yesterday, after we left your village, Robbie, the pilot, went to Juneau and picked up another man. All we know is that he flew away and never came back."

Fleetfoot stared first at Frank, then at Joe, as if trying to read their minds. He said nothing.

"We'd like you to help us find him," Joe

urged. "If you do, I promise he'll give you that ride."

This seemed to convince the Haida lad. "All right," he said slowly. "Fleetfoot believe you." After a short pause, he added, "Me see whirlybird yesterday."

The Hardys' eyes flashed. "You mean you saw it *again,* after we left your village?" Frank asked eagerly.

"Bird fly over village. Go *that* way," the Indian said, pointing northeast.

Joe looked at his brother and whistled. "Toward the Canadian border!"

"Wherever they went, I'll bet Robbie didn't fly there willingly." Frank frowned. "His passenger may have forced him deep into British Columbia. They even may have crashed in the wilderness."

Joe mulled this over. "I think your first guess is right, Frank," he conceded. "This gang we're up against probably doesn't dare take any chances on the police catching up with them. I'll bet they're holding Robbie prisoner."

Frank snapped his fingers. "Do you suppose Mr. Sewell is being held prisoner too—by the same gang?"

"I'll bet you're right," put in Tony. "From what I hear, Mr. Sewell was an experienced woodsman. A tenderfoot might run into trouble in the wilderness, but not an expert who's been working here for years."

Frank went on thoughtfully, "If this gang *is* a foreign group looking for that lost moon rocket, they could probably use a man like Mr. Sewell to help guide them."

"Could be," Joe spoke up. "But for all we know, Robbie's passenger might have been a United States scientist who hired him to make an aerial search for the rocket; or a detective or FBI agent trailing the gang."

Suddenly Frank remembered that Fleetfoot had come with a message. Turning back to the Indian boy, he asked, "What is the news you have for us?"

Fleetfoot smiled proudly. "Me see same two men on river again last night."

"Did you follow them?"

"Fleetfoot follow part way," the boy said. "They go upriver past Devil's Paw into British Columbia. Fleetfoot cannot go there. It is against law for my people to go into Canada. Me think maybe those men break law too. Maybe they steal something and run away."

The Hardys received this new information with keen interest. Frank patted the Indian boy on the shoulder. "Many thanks, Fleetfoot. You've done good work. If you find out anything more, please let us know. And I promise you'll get that whirlybird ride as soon as Robbie shows up!"

The Indian youth grinned. "I find out more, then come back!" He shoved his canoe into the water, leaped aboard nimbly, and waved farewell. *"Klahowya!"*

The boys watched as Fleetfoot paddled across to the mainland with a few deft strokes, then beached the canoe and hoisted it on his head and shoulders for the portage around the falls.

As the Hardys headed back to camp, they considered their next move. "We sure can't cover all this bush country without a helicopter," Frank reasoned. "Our best bet is to return to Juneau to see if we can line up another whirlybird. Maybe the Fish and Wildlife Service can help us."

Joe fell in with this plan, adding, "There might be some news about Robbie, too."

Leaving their canoe on the island with Chet and Tony, the Hardys started back to Juneau in the rented motorboat. The skies, which had been blue and clear when they embarked, gradually darkened with scudding storm clouds.

"We're in for a blow," Joe observed as the water turned leaden gray in color.

"Maybe we can outrun it," Frank said, immediately increasing speed. However, as they left Admiralty Island astern, the wind grew to gale force. It lashed the waves into mountainous breakers, hurling spray high into the air. The Hardys' boat, battered by wind and water, was almost swamped.

Joe bailed frantically. "Can we make shore?" he gasped.

"Not a chance!" Squinting in the teeth of the gale, Frank fought to keep the boat on course. "If we try leaving the channel, we'll pile up on the rocks for sure!"

The rain held off for almost half an hour. Then lightning flashed and a peal of thunder seemed to split the heavens wide open, sending down a drenching torrent.

The boys, already soaked to the skin, redoubled their efforts to keep the boat from swamping. They bailed in shifts, one taking a turn at the wheel while the other scooped out bucket after bucket of water.

The storm pursued them up the Gastineau Channel, but gradually abated as they neared Juneau. Both boys were shivering and utterly exhausted when they finally tied up at the dock. By this time it was past 10 P.M. and almost pitch dark.

"Wow! What a battle!" Joe exclaimed, squeezing water out of his shirt.

"Guess we may as well check in at the hotel," Frank advised. "We can't do anything before morning."

The boys had a hot supper in their room at the Baranof, then turned in and slept until seven the next morning. After a hasty breakfast of bacon and eggs, they hurried down to the seaplane base. When they learned that there was still no news of Robbie Robbins they were disappointed.

"Is there any other copter around here beside Robbie's?" Frank asked the dock guard.

"Not in Juneau," the guard informed them.

"Let's query the Fish and Wildlife Service," Frank suggested. "Perhaps they can get us a whirlybird from Ketchikan or Skagway."

Their visit to the government office, however, proved to be futile.

"Nearest copter's at Anchorage," the agent said. "We tried to charter one ourselves, but the pilot's tied up for the next three weeks."

Before returning to the island, Frank and Joe also checked with Detective Grant at police headquarters. The Hardys told him they planned to search the upper reaches of the Kooniak for traces of the foreign gang, as well as for Sewell and Robbins. "Will we need permission from the Canadian government?" Frank asked.

"Yes," the detective replied, "but I think I can arrange it." Picking up the telephone, he called the Canadian consulate and quickly got an okay. Their permission was extended to include Fleetfoot, as well as Chet and Ted Sewell, in case the latter two decided to accompany the expedition.

"Thanks a lot," Frank told the detective as they shook hands. "One other thing. Can you give us any tips about traveling in British Columbia?"

"Never been up that way myself," Grant replied, "but I'll tell you someone who should know. He's an old-timer named Jess Jenkins. You'll find him at the Alaska Pioneers' Home in Sitka."

The brothers boarded a small commercial plane and within an hour were on the lawn that surrounded the Pioneers' Home in the former Russian capital of Alaska. They found Jess Jenkins sunning himself on a bench in front of the building.

The old fellow proved to be a lean, bewhiskered sourdough who had mined gold in both Canada and Alaska.

"Sure," Jenkins said, when questioned by the young sleuths, "I know what's up there in British Columbia! But I warn you, it's even more dangerous than a hoppin'-mad Kodiak bear!"

CHAPTER X

The Sourdough's Clue

DANGER ahead? Frank and Joe seated themselves on either side of the old sourdough so as not to miss a word of his warning.

"Ah, them was great days," Jenkins reminisced. "We figgered it might pan out almost as rich as Joe Juneau's strike."

The Hardys flashed each other puzzled glances. "What would pan out?" Frank asked. "We don't follow you."

"Why, this gold strike I'm tellin' ye about," Jess replied. "Over into Canady, it was. Seems two fellers come down the Kooniak, luggin' full pokes. Pretty soon the story spread around about them stumblin' on these gravel bars, up some little crick, where the color was runnin' forty dollars to the pan!"

"When was this?" Joe put in.

"Well, let's see. Nigh on fifty years ago, I

reckon." The old sourdough fell silent for a moment. Finally he went on, "Anyhow, folks in Juneau got all het up, hearin' about this new strike. So a bunch o' us boys, we packed up our gear an' hightailed it over into British Columbia to stake out claims."

"What happened?" Frank pressed curiously.

"Trouble, that's what happened!" Jess retorted. "And that's what I'm warnin' you boys about. We found the spot, an' then got chased right out again by a bunch o' wild Injuns!"

"Why?" Joe asked.

" 'Cause this crick where the gold was supposed to be, it run right past a sacred Injun burial ground. Seems as how all their ancestors had been buried there for hundreds an' hundreds o' years. They knew we'd start sinkin' shafts all over the place, an' they didn't take to that idee. So naturally we had to clear out."

"You never went back?" Frank asked.

"Nope. We figgered we'd rather hang onto our scalps fer a while. But some o' our boys got a peek at one o' them graves."

"You mean they dug one up?" Joe said.

"Well, no. What I mean is they got a peek at one o' the grave houses. Little bitty log houses, they are, 'bout six by ten feet. Seems that's where they stored the Injun's weapons an' other gear over his grave. All gone now, I reckon. Ain't even any Injuns livin' in them parts any more."

The old sourdough rambled on, talking about his experiences in the wilds of British Columbia, then the Yukon, and finally reminiscing about various gold camps in Alaska. The Hardys listened attentively, but at last felt they must break away.

"Come again any time, boys," Jess told them, giving each a hearty handshake. "Always glad to talk about the old days!"

Frank and Joe walked away thoughtfully from the Pioneers' Home. "Was there *really* a gold strike up there?" Frank mused.

"Do you doubt it?"

Frank frowned as they walked toward the seaplane basin. "Old Jess said two prospectors came down the Kooniak with full pokes, and a report got spread around about their finding gold. But it could have been an exaggerated story."

"So?"

"Maybe they didn't really strike gold after all. They could have looted those grave houses of valuable Indian jewelry and ornaments."

"And then traded them off for gold?" put in Joe, sensing the drift of his brother's reasoning.

"Yes, and when rumors started about how they made their haul, it touched off a gold rush."

"I'll bet you're right!" Joe said enthusiastically. "That might explain the jade trinket we found in the knapsack!"

"Exactly," Frank agreed. "Furthermore, some-

one may have recently stumbled on the burial
ground again and unearthed more ancient treasure."

They had a half-hour wait for the return
flight to Juneau, so Frank and Joe sat on a bench
at the base of a huge totem pole that overlooked
Sitka Harbor.

"Only one thing doesn't fit in with your theory," Joe said after a few minutes of silence.

"What's that?"

"Where would those old Indians have obtained
jade? It comes from Asia, mostly."

"True enough," Frank said. He added, however, that many scientists believe the Indians
came originally from Asia. If so, they might have
brought their tribal treasures with them.

"In that case," Joe exclaimed excitedly, "the
jade ornament may be valuable scientific evidence!"

Joe's exuberance was interrupted by the distant drone of motors. A plane was arriving from
Juneau and would take off on the return trip in a
few minutes. After the incoming passengers had
debarked, the Hardys took their seats.

Five minutes later the plane was air-borne. It
skimmed over the mountainous islands of the
coast and landed on Gastineau Channel with the
grace of a widgeon. The brothers hastened to the
hotel for their belongings, then purchased a

large quantity of fresh supplies. They hauled them down to the dock, loaded them into the motorboat, and headed back to the island.

On arriving, they found Chet and Tony had been frantic with worry during the night.

"We were afraid you might have cracked up in the storm!" Tony said.

"Besides, we had a scare of our own!" Chet added.

"What happened?" Frank asked.

Tony explained that they had heard the sound of paddles close to the island, shortly after the storm abated. Tony had flashed his searchlight but failed to pick out any canoeists or other boatmen in the darkness.

Joe grinned. "Sure you weren't hearing things?"

"We weren't sure then, but we are now," Chet retorted firmly. He ducked into the pup tent for a moment, and came out holding a well-worn paddle. "Take a look at this. We found it on the beach this morning."

The Hardys examined it. There were no clues to the owner, although the paddle had obviously been hand-carved. "Indian workmanship," Frank speculated. "Perhaps Fleetfoot can identify it."

Then Joe went on to tell of their plan to explore farther along the Kooniak. "We feel sure that the gang must be operating somewhere upriver," he said. "And the only way to find out what they're after is to look for ourselves. I'm hoping we can locate Robbie and Mr. Sewell, too."

Tony received this news with a doubtful expression. "That could be plenty dangerous," he pointed out. "Suppose you run into another ambush?"

"They're not apt to lay a trap for us unless they know we're coming," Frank replied. "If we watch our step and keep our eyes open, we may be able to spot their camp without being seen."

"Especially since we're taking Fleetfoot with us," Joe put in.

"Too bad Ted Sewell isn't here," Frank remarked. "We figured he might want to come along to hunt for his dad."

"Stick around for another twenty-four hours," Tony urged. "Ted ought to show up pretty soon."

The Hardys agreed to wait at least until the following morning. The delay proved worth while since Ted arrived on the island that evening.

As the boys sat around the campfire, Ted reported glumly that he still had had no word on his father. He was amazed to hear about the latest developments in the mystery, and when Frank told about their plans, he eagerly agreed to go up the Kooniak with them.

"I've always wanted to take a trip into British Columbia!" Ted said. "We'll need rifles and ammunition, though. That's bear country!"

Frank and Joe, although their father had carefully trained them in the proper use of firearms, never carried weapons when working on their cases. However, since they had already had two brushes with bears the Hardys could see the wisdom of Ted's words.

"I guess you're right," Frank agreed. "Joe and I don't have guns, though."

"I have a Springfield that I bought from Army surplus," Ted informed them. "Makes a swell hunting rifle! Maybe that'll do for the bunch of us. But you fellows should have some practice before we leave."

After supper, the boys set up a row of empty cans on rocks. Ted then brought out his rifle, which he carried in his boat, as well as several clips of ammunition. To his amazement, both Frank and Joe proved to be excellent marksmen, drilling their target cleanly on every shot.

"You don't need practice!" Ted exclaimed. "You're experts!"

Frank grinned. "I guess Dad's a pretty good teacher."

The rest of the evening was spent in discussing the details of their river trip. It was decided that after picking up Fleetfoot at the Haida village, they would follow the Kooniak at least as far as the Indian grave houses.

The next morning Tony insisted that he would be all right alone on the island. But Chet decided to stay with him. "In case there are any more gun-happy fish poachers around, you'd better have company," the stout boy declared. "I'd probably sink the canoe, anyhow," he added jokingly.

Then Chet suggested they pick some blueberries for breakfast. The others agreed eagerly. So while Tony heaped wood on the campfire and started the bacon frying, the Hardys, Chet, and Ted hiked across the island. On the way Chet suddenly let out a cry of delight.

"Hey, look! Wild celery!" He reached down, pulled up one of the leafy green stalks, and started to bite into it.

Ted paled. "Chet! Stop!" he yelled.

CHAPTER XI

A Fiery Missile

WITH a lightning grab, Ted yanked the stalk out of Chet's mouth before his teeth could sink into it.

"Hey! What's the big idea?" Chet protested.

"That stuff isn't celery," Ted explained. "It's deadly poisonous water hemlock!"

"*P-p-poisonous!*" Chet gulped and clutched his throat. "G-good night! And th-thanks!"

"Don't let it spoil your breakfast," Joe comforted the frightened boy. "We'll pick those blueberries and do some real eating!"

Chet cheered up at this appetizing prospect, and the boys soon returned to camp with a fine haul of berries. After breakfast Tony radioed the Fish and Wildlife Service for news of Robbins and Sewell.

"No word on either of them yet," Tony reported as he took off his earphones. "But the op-

erator passed on a message from the Bayport police."

"What is it?" Joe shouted.

"They've learned that Romo Stransky has a
twin brother named Remo—and *he's* a spy too!"

"Hear that?" Chet crowed triumphantly. "I
told you I wasn't seeing things! Remo must be
the one I saw at Seattle–Tacoma airport!"

"He probably followed us to Juneau, too," Joe
added. "What's more, he may have left one of
those star-and-circle heelmarks here on the island."

Frank went even further with a deduction. "I'll
bet Remo was Robbie's passenger!" The others
agreed. As they prepared for the trip upriver,
Frank went on, "You know, fellows, if we're lucky
enough to find the helicopter, we might be able to
fly it back."

"Suppose the gas tank's empty!" Joe cautioned.

"It most likely will be," Tony said. "But you
could carry enough fuel in the canoe to get the
copter back to Juneau."

Ted Sewell looked doubtful. "The canoe will
be plenty loaded as it is, with all our duffel."

"You're right," Frank agreed. "We'd need an
extra canoe."

"Which means another trip back to Juneau,"
Joe pointed out.

In spite of further delay, Frank's companions
realized his suggestion was a wise one. "Okay,"

Ted said after a short discussion. "We're all in favor. Let's draw straws for the job."

The task fell to Ted and Joe. Embarking in the Hardys' motorboat, they waved good-by and headed up the coast. When they arrived in Juneau, the boys purchased as many tins of gasoline as they felt could be safely carried. On Ted's suggestion, they also stopped at a sportsmen's outfitting store and bought two rifles for Frank and Joe. After the supplies had been loaded aboard, Joe rented another canoe which he fastened to the stern of the motorboat.

As they refreshed themselves with sandwiches and milk at a nearby lunch counter, Joe set his glass down hard.

"Something wrong?" Ted asked.

"Wow!" Joe exclaimed. "Why didn't I think of that before?"

Ted looked baffled. "Of what?"

"The Turner couple Robbie rescued from the glacier," Joe replied in a low voice. "They might have a clue about Robbie's mysterious passenger."

Ted brightened. "That's a smart hunch, Joe! Come on!"

The two boys hurried to the Juneau Hospital, where Joe inquired whether they might see Mr. and Mrs. Turner.

The receptionist nodded pleasantly and consulted the register. "They're in Room 214. You may take the elevator."

In Room 214 Joe and Ted found William Turner in bed, with his leg in a cast. Mrs. Turner, her right arm in a sling, was seated in a chair reading to her husband. Both were delighted to receive visitors.

After Joe had introduced Ted, Mrs. Turner said, "So nice of you boys to come. Where's Frank?"

Joe explained. Then Mr. Turner said, "Hope you boys didn't wait long on the glacier before the pilot returned."

"As a matter of fact, he never did get back," Joe replied.

The couple looked dismayed. "Oh, I'm terribly sorry!" Mr. Turner said. "Robbins *did* develop some kind of trouble on the way into Juneau— with his steering rotor, I think. But he told us it could be fixed."

Joe gave them the details of Robbie's disappearance.

"Oh, dear," exclaimed Mrs. Turner, "I wish we could help!"

"Perhaps you can," said Joe. "Did you notice some clue as to who his passenger was?"

The couple thought in silence. Joe prodded their memory. "Did you see anyone speak to Robbie when you landed at the seaplane base?"

"Only a couple of mechanics who were working on a plane nearby," Mrs. Turner replied. "One of them called an ambulance for us."

Joe then asked whether they had noticed anything suspicious on their glacier expedition.

"I'm afraid not," Turner replied. "You see,
ever since I retired three years ago, Clara and I
have made a hobby of paleontology."

Ted was interested to hear this. "I guess there
are a lot of prehistoric animal bones around our
Alaskan glaciers," he remarked. "I know prospectors have come across the remains of ancient
woolly mammoths. But I've never seen any myself."

Forgetting his unfortunate accident, entirely,
Turner brightened and talked about the finds he
and his wife had made. "As a matter of fact," he
went on, "we believe the earliest life on this planet
developed right here in North America."

"The first human beings too?" Joe asked.

"That's hard to say," Turner replied. "However, I believe the Indians originated on this con-
tinent."

"I thought they were supposed to have come
over from Asia."

"That's the opinion of most scientists," Turner
conceded. "Personally, I think, it was the other
way around. I think they trekked from here to
Asia via the land bridge over the Bering Straits.
Later, there probably was travel back and forth."

"Is there any evidence to support that theory?"
Joe asked.

"Yes, a good deal. There are similarities between the American Indians and Asiatics both in features and customs. Also, they both used the bow and arrow, and have many common root words in their languages."

Excitedly now, Joe queried, "How about their ornaments and jewelry? Is there any chance the Alaskan Indians might have brought jade carvings back from Asia?"

Mr. Turner nodded. "Very possible, I should say." After hearing about the boys' planned trip up the Kooniak River, he said, "Why not keep alert for traces of prehistoric animals? You might stumble on some valuable finds."

"What should we look for?" Ted inquired.

"Well, a white streak in gray rock might indicate a bone fossil," Turner replied. "Or a depression in the rock could be a dinosaur's footprint. Either one could lead you to a prehistoric skeleton."

"We'll remember that!" Joe promised, as the boys got ready to leave.

They quickly strode to the dock and shoved off in the heavily laden motorboat, with the canoe trailing behind.

As soon as the two boys reached the island, Joe told Frank of the conversation at the hospital. Frank was pleased to learn that the Turners supported his theory about the jade piece.

Not long after supper, the boys turned in, hoping for a good night's sleep before embarking up the Kooniak next morning. Soon the camp was wrapped in silence.

But Frank was restless. Turning and tossing in his sleeping bag, he kept reviewing in his mind the baffling events that had happened since the Hardys had arrived in Alaska.

As the object struck the dock

"Were those fish poachers mixed up in this mystery?" he wondered. "And what about Robbie? . . . Looking for that gang in this wilderness may turn out to be a lot more than we bargained for."

Unable to sleep, Frank rose and pulled on his

it exploded with a dull thud

slacks, socks, and loafers. The luminous hands on his watch pointed to 12:20. He strolled toward the water, listening to the sighing of the night breeze in the tall pines.

Suddenly another sound broke the stillness— the soft plash of an oar, then a *clink* of metal containers rattling against one another! Frank strained his eyes in the darkness, every sense alert. The next second he shouted:

"Wake up, fellows! Someone's stealing our canoe and gasoline!"

As Frank raced toward the dock, Joe, Chet, Ted, and Tony burst out of their tents and sprinted in their bare feet. Too late! The noise of a motor roaring into action told them the intruder was making a clean getaway!

Reaching the water's edge, Frank saw their canoe and gasoline untouched! The raider's boat kicked up a violent wake as it streaked off. Suddenly the strange man stood upright and hurled something toward the island. As the object struck the little wooden dock next to the canoe, it burst with a dull thud and yellow flames shot high into the air!

Frank's face blanched in the blinding glare. "It's a fire bomb!" he yelled.

CHAPTER XII

Dinosaur Detective

"TONY, get our axes!" Frank commanded as the dock burst into flame. To the others he cried, "Follow me!"

As Tony dashed back to camp, Frank kicked off his loafers and plunged into the water. With his jackknife, he slashed the lines holding the boats.

"Chet, take our motorboat! Ted, pilot yours!"

Joe, meanwhile, was frantically attaching the canoes by towlines to the crafts. "Okay! Take off!"

Chet and Ted revved up their motors and sped into the middle of the river. The Hardys, seared by the heat from the fiery dock, beached Tony's boat at a safe distance, then hastily scrambled ashore.

Tony was already hacking at the dock timbers. "There's an axe and a hatchet for you fellows!" he called.

Half the wooden structure was a crackling mass

101

of flames. Shielding their faces as best they could, the three boys quickly cut away the remaining supports. Then Frank levered up the planking with his axe.

"Okay! Into the water!" he gasped.

Straining every muscle the trio ripped up the flimsy structure and hurled it into the water. It sank with a hissing cloud of steam. Panting and streaked with perspiration, the boys watched as the flames died out.

"Wow!" Tony muttered. "If that fire had spread to the brush, our whole camp would have gone up in smoke!"

Once the danger of an explosion was past, Chet and Ted returned with the boats and canoes. These were moored to the blackened stumps of the dock pilings. Then all of the boys trudged back to camp.

"Good thing you were awake, Frank," Ted remarked wryly.

"We should have kept up our night watches," Joe added. "Tony, I think you and Chet need more protection after we three leave the island."

"At least," Frank concurred, "report what happened right away."

"I'll do it now," Tony replied.

Warming up his radio, Tony tuned to the agency's special frequency and spoke into the microphone: "Kooniak calling Juneau! . . . Can you read me?"

Fortunately, the station kept an operator on duty around the clock. After hearing Tony's report of the fire-bomb attack, he consulted his superiors by telephone, and then called back. "We'll send out two men first thing in the morning!"

Much relieved, the five boys drank some hot cocoa which Chet had brewed. Ted volunteered to stand the first watch during the remaining hours of darkness. Then the others crawled into their sleeping bags. The rest of the night passed quietly.

Shortly before ten o'clock the next morning a boat arrived at the island, bringing the two agents from Juneau. They came ashore, carrying a small but powerful two-way radio set, which they turned over to the Hardys.

"The chief thought this might come in handy on your trip up the Kooniak," one of the men explained. "If you get a lead on the gang, he'd like you to report to Juneau at once."

"Thanks. We'll do that," Frank promised.

Half an hour later the Hardy brothers and Ted set off, paddling to the western shore of the river. Here they unloaded the two canoes and made the portage around the falls.

"Whew! That's a full day's work before we even get started!" Joe remarked, wiping the perspiration from his brow.

Ted chuckled. "These Alaskan rivers are beautiful, but you'll find they're no picnic!"

After a brief lunch the boys embarked on the next leg of their journey. Frank volunteered to paddle the trailing canoe which carried the gasoline cans.

Ted approved. "We'll ride better that way, with one man behind. And there'll be no danger of losing the fuel tins in an upset."

Ted himself, as the most experienced woodsman of the trio, took the bow position in the lead canoe. They shoved off, and soon found themselves paddling against a swift current. They were also traveling "uphill," since the Kooniak flowed down from the Alaskan coastal range.

"Boy, looks as though we're in for a real workout!" Joe called back to his brother. Frank grinned in response.

"Don't worry, you two are in good shape," Ted commented. "This would be rough for a tenderfoot."

At points along the riverbanks the heavy timber thinned out into lush meadowlands. These were carpeted with wild flowers in every color of the rainbow. Frank and Joe were amazed at the dazzling display.

"It's like a giant garden!" Joe said admiringly.

Ted pointed out many of the species by name —alpine forget-me-nots, fireweed with its tall reddish spires, yellow Arctic poppies, bluebells, creeping dogwood, and purple irises.

Steering close to shore, he reached out and

plucked several flowers from a mass of yellow blooms that grew down to the water's edge. "Monkey flowers," he told Joe."

"They do look like little faces," Joe said with a chuckle.

After paddling for several hours, they reached an area where the banks of the Kooniak rose in rocky walls. The beetling cliffs formed a canyon for the swift-flowing icy waters.

"Hey, look!" Joe cried suddenly, pointing up at one of the cliff faces. "There's a white streak in the rock! I'll bet it's part of a dinosaur!"

When Joe suggested investigating the streak, Ted and Frank agreed to moor the canoe and accompany him.

"It'll be a tough climb, though," Ted warned.

"We can make it!" Joe urged enthusiastically.

Mooring their canoes to a clump of rock, the boys climbed out and began scaling the cliff. Footholds were few. After skinning their arms and legs on the rugged outcroppings, they finally reached the whitish streak.

"I'm sure it's a bone!" Joe exclaimed.

All three examined it closely.

"Could be," Ted agreed. "But how do we get it out?"

"By the Indian method," Frank suggested. "Chip it loose with a sharp stone."

Arming themselves with chunks of flint, the boys followed Frank's suggestion. For a while they seemed to make little impression on the rock face. But gradually more of the white object became revealed.

"I was right!" Joe exclaimed. "It's definitely a bone!"

"Looks like some kind of an elbow or knee joint," Ted commented. "If dinosaurs had such things!"

"Wait'll I get back and tell Mr. Turner about this find!" Joe said jubilantly.

Frank broke into a chuckle. "I bet they'll give you a medal!" he joked. "It'll be engraved to Joe Hardy—finder of a dinosaur's funny bone!"

Both Joe and Ted joined in the laughter. However, as the boys started down toward the canoes, their smiles faded. The steep cliff, which had been so difficult to climb, seemed almost impossible to descend.

Suddenly Joe gasped as he lost his footing. With a yell, he slid downward, making frantic attempts to slow his descent.

CHAPTER XIII

A Savage Ordeal

TED acted instantly! Leaping out from the cliff, he dived into the water far below. Then, after a few strong strokes, Ted reached the rocky shore and climbed to the foot of the slope.

Joe, tumbling and twisting, was almost at the bottom of the cliff. Timing the descent perfectly, Ted caught hold of Joe, breaking his fall just short of a jagged rock formation.

The impact threw both boys to the flinty ground, where they panted and trembled for a few moments.

"Whew!" gasped Joe finally. "How can I thank you, Ted! Finding that dinosaur bone came close to killing me! If it hadn't been for you, my own bones would be in pretty bad shape by now!"

"Just a lucky catch," Ted said with a grin.

Even so, Joe had suffered many bruises and his skin was scraped raw in several places.

Frank, who had tensely watched the rescue, shouted his thanks to Ted and added, "I'll find a safer part of the cliff to come down!"

By climbing higher and crossing a shelf of rock to a point farther upriver, he was able to make the descent in safety.

Ted, meanwhile, had opened their first-aid kit and applied medication to Joe's cuts.

"I never knew fossil hunting could be so dangerous!" Frank quipped wryly as he rejoined the other two. "Guess we should have learned our lesson from that trip out West with Cap Bailey!"

Frank was referring to a fossil-hunting expedition which had led him and Joe into a life-or-death struggle with a band of train robbers. The Hardys listed the case in their files as *The Secret of Wildcat Swamp*.

"You can say that again!" Joe muttered, blowing on a particularly painful cut on his right knee. "Wow! Does that sting!"

After resting for fifteen minutes, the trio resumed the trip upriver. Although they watched both banks of the river carefully, the boys saw no one, white man or Indian. Nor did they sight any traces of a recent camp.

Toward evening they approached a small, wooded island in mid-river. "Getting hungry?" Frank inquired.

"If we don't eat soon," Joe replied, "I'll start gnawing on this paddle!"

"Then let's camp here," Frank suggested. "It should make a pretty safe spot for the night."

After paddling into a small cove, the travelers beached the canoes and scouted the island thoroughly before unloading their gear.

Soon a campfire was crackling and the aroma of hot corned beef and fried potatoes drifted over the island. After supper the companions chose watch periods. Joe drew the first assignment. Frank and Ted stretched out in their sleeping bags and were soon deep in slumber. All were thoroughly refreshed by daybreak, although Joe was still somewhat stiff and sore.

Breakfast over, the canoeists pushed on. The river lay under a light blanket of mist, not yet burned away by the sun. Several hours of paddling brought them to an open spot on the west bank, where the clustering pines gave way to a narrow clearing.

"Hold it!" Ted cried, signaling with his paddle. "That's an Indian trail!"

"It might lead to the Haida camp," Joe conjectured.

Frank felt certain of this. "Let's go ashore and get Fleetfoot," he urged.

"Think our gear will be safe here?" Joe asked, as they drew the canoes up on the riverbank.

"Better not take any chances," Frank replied. "I vote we cache our supplies and each of the canoes in a separate spot."

Joe and Ted concurred, and in twenty minutes the boys had everything well hidden under heaps of brush and rocks. Then they headed inland along the trail. Soon they came upon an Indian village.

As they neared the cluster of wooden huts, excited noises reached their ears. A crowd of Indians were swarming about the village clearing.

The boys stopped short in astonishment at an amazing sight. A native woman, wearing a green fringed parka, shot straight upward at least thirty feet above the crowd! She was treading air to remain upright!

Seconds later, she landed on both feet in a walrus skin held by six Indians. They immediately snapped the hide taut and catapulted her up in the air again!

"Good night!" Joe gasped. "What do they think she is—a human medicine ball?"

A slender young Indian turned at the sound of Joe's voice. It was Fleetfoot. He ran toward them with a wide-eyed look of fear. "Quick! Do not let my people see you!" he whispered. "Run for your lives!"

The boys looked puzzled, and Frank said, "Why? Your tribe was friendly enough the other time we came to your village."

"Today we are having a wedding," Fleetfoot explained. "That woman is the bride. She is a Kotzebue Eskimo, and now she is proving to everyone that she will be a good, *skookum* wife!"

"By letting them bounce her on that walrus hide?" Joe asked.

Fleetfoot nodded impatiently. "It is a custom of her people. And today any outsiders who come here must do the same! But it takes much practice. If they bounce you like that, you will break your neck!"

"Wow!" Ted gulped. "We'd better clear out of here! Come on!"

But the boys had tarried too long. Hearing their voices, the Indians swarmed toward them excitedly. Before the Hardys and Ted could take to their heels, they were dragged into the circle of yelling, whooping Haidas!

"Now white man try test!" shouted one tall Indian. The others approved with grins and handclaps.

"Hey, wait a minute!" Frank pleaded, striving to make himself heard above the uproar. "We just came here as visitors, to see one of your people. We didn't know there was a wedding going on!"

Fleetfoot confirmed this. He jabbered excitedly in the Haida tongue, trying to persuade his fellow Indians to let the white youths go. But the tall man swept him aside.

"White men come to village, they must join in wedding games too!" the brave asserted. He pointed to Frank. "This one biggest, look plenty *skookum*. He try test with walrus hide!"

The brave explained the rules of the game. Frank would be bounced in the air three times. If he failed to land upright after three tries, he would be made to jump through a circle of burning arrows.

Frank stared at the speaker unbelievingly. "This is crazy!" he thought. "They can't really mean it!" But one look at the circle of intense coppery faces told him they were not jesting. For the moment at least, the Haidas had reverted to the savage customs of the Alaskan wilderness!

Smothering the protests of Joe, Ted, and Fleetfoot, the Indians seized Frank and hustled him onto the walrus hide. Then the hide was raised aloft and snapped taut. Frank went hurtling high in the air!

He tried frantically to tread air with his hands and feet as he had seen the Eskimo woman do. But the dizzying momentum of his flight upward seemed to rob him of his sense of balance. Twisting helplessly, Frank plummeted back toward the walrus hide and landed on his back with jarring force.

Stunned, Frank struggled to his feet. The Indians gave him a moment's respite, then again hurled him aloft!

Joe and Ted watched, wide-eyed and helpless. For a second, Frank seemed to be dancing on air. Then, thrashing violently, he came down again, this time landing on one side.

Frank was hurtled high in the air

Badly shaken, Frank managed to stand up. His last chance! Although his heart was hammering, Frank gritted his teeth, determined not to fail. Once more the Indians catapulted him into the air.

Joe could scarcely bear to watch. Ted clutched his arm in breathless suspense.

Arrowing straight upward, Frank closed his eyes, keeping his arms close to his sides. As he reached his highest point in mid-air, he opened his eyes again. The circle of Indians stood far below, gaping up at him, the walrus hide seeming not much bigger than a handkerchief.

Suddenly Frank felt himself begin to fall, slowly at first, then at elevator speed. He stretched out his arms and trod the air gently with his feet, like a man on a unicycle. It worked! He landed squarely on both feet, still upright!

The crowd roared its approval! Frank was lifted off the walrus hide, hoisted onto the shoulders of two Indians, and paraded about the village clearing amid whoops and yells.

"You *skookum* fella!" the Haida chief beamed at Frank when he was finally allowed to stand on his own feet again. "Now you and two friends all come to wedding feast!"

"Thanks," Frank replied, a trifle weakly. Joe and Ted, then Fleetfoot, wrung his hand in congratulation.

"Terrific!" Joe told his brother.

"I just kept thinking of those flaming arrows."
Frank grinned. "That's what did it."

"It's a wonder you could think at all after those
first two jolts!" Ted exclaimed.

The villagers now gathered about a great cen-
tral campfire. Two medicine men performed a
religious dance, then the chief joined the hands
of the Indian groom and his Eskimo bride. The
wedding feast followed.

Squaws brought around huge carved wooden
platters heaped with food. The first course con-
sisted of slabs of pink salmon.

"Good night! It's raw!" Joe whispered.

The boys took some, however, in order not to
offend their hosts, and managed to eat a few bites.
The bear steaks and stewed rabbit which followed
were more to their liking. These were accompanied by nuts, berries, vegetables, and fruits,
including one with a citrus flavor, which tasted
like a cross between lemon and grapefruit. Ted
identified it as the fruit of the wild rose.

"Boy, now we're getting fancy!" Joe chuckled
as he sampled the fruit's delicate flavor. "Hmm!
Not bad, though!"

There was also a sort of coarse baked bread.
"Wonder what it's made out of?" Frank muttered,
after trying a few bites.

Fleetfoot explained, "Women make flour by
grinding up bulbs of rice lily." He pointed to
some brownish-purple flowers which several of

the squaws wore in their hair. "Those are flowers from same plant."

When the feast was over, the Hardys at last found an opportunity to tell Fleetfoot about their trip upriver. Frank asked if the Indian youth would accompany them as guide.

"I glad to come with you!" he explained. "But I take my own canoe. It is much better than white man's."

"Fine! Let's go!" said Joe.

But Fleetfoot looked shocked. "No, no!" he told the boys. "Cannot go now. Wedding party is just beginning!"

"Just beginning?" Frank echoed uneasily.

"Still much dancing, singing to come," Fleetfoot explained. "You wait. We go tomorrow morning."

The Hardys and Ted looked questioningly at one another, trying to conceal their feelings of impatience at the further delay. However, there was nothing to do but yield. Settling back, they prepared to watch the proceedings.

Soon tom-toms beat. The medicine men started a slow, stately dance, shaking wooden rattles. As the tempo increased, the other Indians joined in and the squaws chanted steadily. The three visitors found themselves absorbed in the ceremony, despite the delay in their journey.

"Whew!" Joe exclaimed in wonderment. "How long can they keep on dancing?"

Fleetfoot smiled broadly. "Oh—Indians love dance. Never get tired."

Gradually, as shadows gathered in the forest, the white boys became drowsy. One by one, Joe, Ted, and Frank all dropped off to sleep.

When they awoke, it was daylight. Fleetfoot was shaking them. "Come! We start now!" he said.

Returning to the river, the Hardys and Ted uncovered the gear which they had cached. The supplies were loaded aboard, and the canoes launched in the water.

Fleetfoot disappeared long enough to get his own birchbark canoe, which was beached farther downstream. In a few minutes he came into sight, paddling with smooth, graceful strokes.

As he drew alongside, Frank said, "There's something we meant to ask you, Fleetfoot. The other night a carved wooden paddle was washed up on our island at the mouth of the river." When Frank described the shape of it, a strange expression of fear and awe passed over Fleetfoot's face!

CHAPTER XIV

A Suspicious Campsite

"FLEETFOOT looks as if he's seen a ghost," Frank thought.

The Indian boy quickly regained his composure and asked slowly, "Did paddle have cuts in handle?"

"Yes," Joe spoke up. "Two small rounded gouges."

Fleetfoot fairly trembled. His eyes grew wide. "That paddle made before white man came! Even before my grandfather's grandfather was born!"

"You mean back in the days of the ancient Athapascan Indians?" Ted asked.

"Yes! Yes! Paddle left on beach by spirit of old Indian!"

"I doubt it," said Frank thoughtfully.

"So do I," Joe chimed in. "There were live men paddling around the island that night. Probably the same bunch we're looking for. Most likely one of them had seen that symbol somewhere and copied it for good luck."

Frank agreed with this theory. "They probably saw a paddle like that when they robbed the Indian grave houses," he remarked to Joe in an undertone. "Stop to think of it, that may be where the paddle came from!"

Ted was eager to push on, so they started upriver. This time, Joe rode the trailing canoe which carried the cans of fuel.

As they penetrated deeper into the interior, the country became increasingly wilder. At times they saw deer push out of the tangled underbrush to drink at the water's edge. Once they surprised a brown bear fishing in rocky shallows, but the beast, startled, hastily withdrew into the forest.

After pausing briefly for lunch, they continued their journey upstream. Frank and Joe, whose arm muscles had ached at the end of the first day's canoeing, gradually found themselves swinging their paddles with the same smooth, easy rhythm as Ted Sewell and Fleetfoot.

Presently Ted pointed ahead to their left. "There's Devil's Paw!" he called out.

The weird outcropping of rock loomed against the mountainous sky line like four fingers and a thumb sticking up in the air.

Fleetfoot paddled close to the other canoes. "This is bad place," he confided. "Old men of my tribe say devil carved it from rock. Indians not go there."

"In that case," Joe mused, "it would make a perfect hide-out for the gang. Indians would stay away from it, and the average white man would have no reason for going there."

Frank nodded. "You're right. We'd better investigate."

At first Fleetfoot objected, but as soon as he realized that the boys were not frightened by the old Indian tales, he lost his fear. Moreover, the prospect of stalking criminals filled him with keen anticipation. His Indian blood rose to the challenge.

"If bad men there, Fleetfoot find 'um!" he vowed.

Running their canoes ashore, the searchers cached their crafts and provisions for a second time.

"Take your rifles," Ted advised tersely. Each of them shoved a clip of cartridges into the magazine of his firearm and stuffed more into pockets before setting off on the rugged trek toward Devil's Paw.

Their present point on the Kooniak, Ted said, was three thousand feet above sea level. All about them, pine and spruce trees were still plentiful, but the riverbanks had become increasingly rocky and precipitous. As a result, hiking was difficult.

Carrying their rifles in one hand and clutching at trees and shrubs with the other, the four made their way up the steep slope. From time to time one of them missed his footing, sending a shower of rocks and gravel clattering toward the river.

"We'll never take the gang by surprise at this rate!" Joe grumbled, pausing to wipe the sweat from his eyes.

After half an hour of hard climbing, they reached a point where Devil's Paw and the entire surrounding terrain stood out in clear view. But there was no sign of a campfire, nor any other trace of human beings.

"Maybe we've been wasting our time," Ted said, discouraged.

"We can't be sure," Frank replied, "without making a closer search." Now, however, the approaches were so steep that it was impossible to climb farther.

Tired and disheartened, the boys retraced their route to the canoes.

"If the gang really is using Devil's Paw for a hide-out," Ted remarked, "they must have some easier way of getting to it."

"Right," Joe nodded, removing a pebble from his shoe. "There must be a secret trail somewhere."

Fleetfoot spoke up eagerly. "You wait here. Me go look for trail."

"Hey! Wait!" Frank called out.

The boy did not seem to hear. He darted nimbly up the mountainside, and was soon lost to view among the scrub evergreens and underbrush.

Frank, Joe, and Ted waited, sprawled comfortably on spongy pine needles among the rocks. All were glad of a chance to rest. As time passed, however, they gradually became uneasy. More than an hour had gone by since Fleetfoot's departure. Minute after minute ticked away, with still no sign of the Indian boy.

"Wonder what's keeping him?" Frank glanced at his watch for what seemed like the hundredth time.

"Let's hope he didn't stumble into the gang," Joe remarked. He greatly admired the high-spirited Indian, and by now was thoroughly alarmed for his safety.

"We should have given him one of the rifles," Ted added gloomily.

The words were hardly spoken before the underbrush parted and Fleetfoot stepped into view, a wide grin on his coppery face.

"Me find trail," he reported proudly. "Ground show many footprints. Look like men go back and forth many times!"

"How about their camp?" Joe asked eagerly. "Did you find where the trail led?"

"Me find camp. But no one there—strangers all gone away. We get in canoes, go on up river," he urged. "Then we look here again on way back."

Frank and Joe rejected this suggestion. Being good detectives, they were determined to follow through on their plan, leaving no stone unturned in their search for clues.

"You've done fine, Fleetfoot," Frank told him. "But we'd like a look at that campsite ourselves. Will you take us to it?"

Fleetfoot agreed willingly, and after gathering up their rifles, the three white youths followed him. Fleetfoot led them upriver for a short distance, following a twisting route among the trees and rocks. Then he turned left, up a narrow draw.

"Now you see trail." Fleetfoot pointed to a well-beaten path. It sloped gently up the mountainside by easy stages.

"Nice work, Fleetfoot!" Joe congratulated him. Bending close to the ground, he added, "Frank, here are more of those star-and-circle heelmarks!"

Pressing forward up the trail, they found the campsite. It lay at the base of one finger of Devil's Paw. Here again were many of the odd heelprints, as well as the blackened ashes of a recent campfire. A number of empty, discarded food cans had also been tossed carelessly aside.

"Pretty sure nobody would ever find this spot, weren't they?" Joe commented.

"Are you sure none of the gang is lurking around?" Ted asked Fleetfoot.

"No one here," he replied confidently. "Me scout for strangers before I come up trail."

"The question now," Frank put forth, "is whether they're coming back? And if so, how soon?"

"Let's take a look around while we're up here," Joe suggested. "We might spot a smoking campfire."

Joe led the way as they followed the shelf-like rock which rimmed the base of Devil's Paw. The ground sloped away below in a steep, brush-covered incline.

Rounding a corner of the weird finger-and-thumb rock formation, Joe stopped suddenly and looked down. "Hey! Come here quick!" he yelled to the others, beckoning frantically.

CHAPTER XV

The Singing Wilderness

STARTLED by his brother's shout, Frank looked up, barely in time to see Joe suddenly drop out of sight.

"Oh, no!" Frank exclaimed. Fleetfoot and Ted rushed to his side, then all three climbed to the spot where Joe had just been standing.

In utter amazement they stared down a long, rocky slope. *At the bottom lay a helicopter.* Joe was scrambling toward it.

Near the edge of a barren, desolate area of forest-tufted rock formations, the wide-spreading branches of a tall cedar effectively concealed the craft from the air. The boys' vantage point, however, gave them an unobstructed view.

"Come on, fellows!" Joe yelled up the steep mountainside. "Let's see if Robbie's anywhere around!"

Frank, Ted, and Fleetfoot all followed eagerly.

Grabbing for a handhold on any rock or clump of shrubbery that offered a grip, they made their way down the incline at breakneck speed.

Joe was already examining the helicopter as they approached. "The fuel tank's empty," he reported. "No sign of Robbie, either."

A weird silence lay over the desolate scene. Except for a hawk circling overhead, there was no other sign of life. While Ted and Fleetfoot watched curiously, the Hardys subjected the helicopter to a careful scrutiny.

"At least there's no blood or signs of a struggle," Joe commented. "That may mean Robbie is still safe."

Frank asked Ted and Fleetfoot to stand guard over the helicopter while he and Joe investigated the surrounding wilderness for clues. "Keep an eye up there toward Devil's Paw," he added, "in case any of the gang comes back."

"Okay," Ted replied. "You fellows watch your step, too. If any of that bunch *are* around, they might try to spring an ambush."

Gripping their rifles firmly, the Hardys began combing the terrain around the helicopter in widening circles. The silence was broken only by the scuffing sound of their footsteps among the brush and gravel. A lone birdcall suddenly echoed among the pines, then died away in a twitter.

"Boy, this place is eerie!" Joe muttered.

"It's hard to believe *any* human being was ever here before us!" Frank said.

Not a footprint or broken twig gave the slightest indication of recent visitors to the area. Overhead, the hawk was still soaring and circling in search of prey.

Suddenly Frank stopped short and clutched his brother's arm. "Joe!" he hissed. "Do you hear something—or am I imagining things?"

"Hear what?" Joe inquired. Then his questioning look gave way to an expression of blank amazement. "It's *music!*"

The strains of a dance orchestra wafted faintly through the wilderness!

"Must be a radio playing somewhere," Joe said finally.

"But where?"

Stiffly tense, the brothers looked cautiously about. Were members of the gang hidden nearby, watching every movement? Was a trap about to be sprung on them? Hearts pounding and eyes alert, Frank and Joe walked on, holding their rifles cradled at the ready. They poked into the underbrush and peered among the trees.

"The sounds are coming from over there," Frank said, pointing to a formation of granite boulders.

The boys approached cautiously, fearful of a possible trap. They scouted around the rocks, but saw nobody. Neither was there any sign of a radio.

"Ether ghosts!" Joe exclaimed, mystified. "The wilderness is singing to us."

Abruptly the music died away. A few seconds later the Hardys were electrified to hear a voice speak clearly in a foreign language! But neither Frank nor Joe could identify any of the words.

Then a second voice replied—this time in English: "The salmon are going up the river. The bears will have a feast." As the voice finished speaking, the music resumed.

"What do you make of it?" Joe asked his brother, completely baffled.

Suddenly an idea occurred to Frank. "Wait a second! Let's check some of these other rocks!"

The brothers put their ears to several boulders. All were broadcasting the music. Frank snapped his fingers excitedly.

"Joe, I've got it! Somehow these rocks are acting as natural receivers and picking up a broadcast signal! I've read about cases like this before! Remember that man in Newark who picked up broadcasts in the fillings of his teeth? It nearly drove him crazy."

"That must be the answer," Joe agreed. "But I still don't understand how it happens."

"Neither do I, exactly," Frank admitted. "It has something to do with their resonating frequency, I guess, just like a crystal detector. Maybe there's something about these rocks that intensi-

fies the signals, too. Anyhow, I think we're getting the gang's broadcast."

"No doubt about that," Joe replied. "The
voices that broke in didn't sound like commercial
broadcasters or ordinary radio hams!"

"Those words in English must have been in
code," Frank went on.

"You're right!" Joe exclaimed. He conjectured
further about the radio reference to salmon. "It
ties in with what Fleetfoot overheard on the
river."

"And," Frank said thoughtfully, "I didn't like
the remark about the bears having a feast."

"What do you mean?"

"The salmon going upriver may refer to us,"
Frank explained. "And 'the bears will have a
feast' could mean our enemies are laying a trap."

"Good night!" Joe stared at his brother in dismay. "That makes sense, all right! But what can
we do about it?"

Frank shrugged. "Just keep our guard up, I
guess. Come on," he added. "Let's go back."

By the time the Hardys returned to the helicopter, the music had ceased. But Ted Sewell and
the Indian lad were still tense with alarm at the
strange sounds of the "singing wilderness." They,
too, had heard the broadcast, although much
more faintly than Frank and Joe. Fleetfoot was
particularly frightened at what seemed to him to
be spirit noises.

"Devil's Paw is bad place, I tell you!" he kept repeating. "Evil spirits live here!"

Frank reassured him, explaining the strange phenomenon as best he could. Fortunately, Fleetfoot had listened to the portable radios of white sportsmen on several occasions, and the Hardys were finally able to convince him that this was just another broadcast.

"How about the camp up there?" Joe asked. "Any signs that the gang might be coming back?"

Ted shook his head. "Not so far. But, you know, there's one thing I can't figure out."

"What's that?"

"How come the copter's fuel tank is empty? Robbie couldn't have figured out beforehand how much he'd need to fly here."

"That's a good point, Ted," Frank lauded him. "I have a hunch they must have drained off the gas to keep anyone from flying the helicopter away. Maybe there's a can of it hidden around here somewhere."

They searched the brush and examined the ground for any sign of digging, but all in vain.

"Well, what'll we do with the copter?" Joe asked finally. "Gas it up and try flying to Juneau?"

"Not yet," Frank urged. "We've more sleuthing to do before we crack this mystery. If the gang found the whirlybird gone, they'd be on the alert. I vote we go upriver a bit and pick up the copter on our way back."

The others agreed to this plan. Returning to their canoes, the boys unloaded the fuel cans which they had brought along and buried them in a well-hidden cache. Then they embarked once more and continued their journey upstream.

As they paddled along, the four watched both shores of the river like hawks, alert for the slightest sign of movement. But the wilderness lay steeped in brooding silence.

When evening approached, the searchers beached their canoes and made camp in a spot well sheltered by firs and tall brush. On Fleetfoot's suggestion, they avoided lighting a campfire. After a cold supper of canned meat loaf and potato salad, they chose watches and prepared to turn in.

Some time later, Frank, Joe, and Ted were quietly awakened by Fleetfoot. Except for a glimmer of moonlight through the evergreens, the river lay shrouded in darkness. A chill night breeze was blowing down from the mountains.

"What's up, Fleetfoot?" Frank asked, instantly alert.

The Indian youth put his finger to his lips, then whispered, "Look over there, across river!"

The Hardys and Ted stared intently, their hearts pounding with excitement.

Lights flickered on the opposite shore!

CHAPTER XVI

An Eerie Sight

"THE gang!" Ted gasped as the four stared at the moving lights across the river.

"Sure aren't fireflies!" Joe stated tersely. "How about it, Frank? Should we paddle over and see what they're up to?"

Frank pondered the situation with a worried frown. "If we try it, we may give ourselves away," he pointed out.

"We have rifles," Ted argued.

Frank shook his head. "We want to avoid any shooting."

"Suppose we go back downriver where they can't spot us, and cross over?" Joe suggested. "Then we could sneak up on the other side and take them by surprise."

"It might work," Frank admitted.

"Unless they hear us hauling the canoe," Ted cautioned.

The boys conversed in low tones, discussing various plans. Fleetfoot finally settled the question by saying that he could paddle silently across the stream and scout the area without being detected. Knowing the young Indian's skill at canoeing and woodcraft, the boys agreed.

"No worry," Fleetfoot whispered. "When Indian not want to be seen, no one see 'um. Me come back soon!"

"Don't take any chances!" Frank told him.

The Hardys and Ted watched the Haida lad creep through the underbrush. Keeping low, he reached the water's edge and slid his birchbark canoe noiselessly into the water. Then he slipped aboard and paddled out into midstream with smooth, silent strokes. In a few moments his ghostly figure melted from view in the darkness.

Tense moments passed. "He should be there by now," Frank whispered.

Suddenly the twinkling lights vanished as if turned off by a master switch. "Leapin' catfish!" Joe muttered. "They must have spotted Fleetfoot!"

"Don't jump to conclusions," Frank said calmly. "Perhaps the gang moved farther into the woods."

Joe and Ted alternately worried about whether Fleetfoot had been captured. Frank tried to allay their fears with a jest. "That would leave us up the creek without an Indian," he whispered.

Twenty minutes later, however, Frank inwardly felt a growing concern. The situation would certainly be even more perilous without Fleetfoot.

Suddenly, just as silently as he had left, Fleetfoot reappeared at the side of his comrades. Ted jumped with surprise and stared openmouthed.

"Boy! It's good to see you!" Frank said. "What happened?"

"Me see four men," the Haida reported. "They carry lights to search for something."

"The lost moon rocket!" Joe exclaimed excitedly.

"Could be," Frank said. "Did you hear anything they were saying, Fleetfoot?"

The Indian lad shook his head. "No, they keep quiet, not talk at all. Fleetfoot think they must sleep in daytime, hunt only at night. That way, run no danger from bears, and no one ask questions."

"You're probably right," Frank said. "Do they have a boat?"

"No boat," Fleetfoot replied. "Me look all along shore, see nothing."

"How about Robbie Robbins, the man who flies the whirlybird?" Joe asked. "Was he with them?"

Again Fleetfoot shook his head. "No. Man who flies whirlybird is young and tall. These men older. Not so tall."

"Then my dad couldn't be one of them, either," Ted put in quietly. "He's six-foot-two."

Thoroughly aroused by the events of the past hour, the boys were too wide awake to think of crawling back into their sleeping bags. For the next few minutes they excitedly discussed the mysterious goings-on across the river. Frank and Joe's conviction grew stronger that the ghostly search party might be looking for traces of the fallen moon rocket.

After listening with keen interest, Fleetfoot suggested that they break camp immediately and push on upriver.

"Why?" Ted queried. "Do you think those men suspected we were over here?"

Fleetfoot shrugged. "Me not know. But maybe they find out in morning. Then we have trouble."

"Fleetfoot's right," said Frank. "It'll be safer to clear out now, before they get wise to us. Come on! Let's head for those Indian grave houses. I have a hunch that's where we'll find the real key to this mystery!"

The others agreed. After putting on their clothes and rolling up their sleeping bags, the boys piled their gear back in the canoes. Ted had already been informed of Jess Jenkins' story about the ancient Indian burial ground. Before shoving off, the Hardys also related the story to Fleetfoot.

"Me hear about that place." He nodded. "Fleetfoot like to see. I help you find it."

"You've already helped us a lot," Frank said gratefully, clapping the young Indian on the back.

Once again the Haida boy broke into his infectious grin. "You right," he agreed proudly. "Fleetfoot *skookum* Injun!"

The four now carefully covered all traces of their camp with leaves and brush. Then they launched their canoes in the water and quickly climbed in. Soon they were paddling upriver through the darkness at a brisk clip.

Dawn found the canoeists many miles farther up the Kooniak. Halting for breakfast, they decided to refresh themselves first with a swim.

"Br-r-r! It's a regular ice bath!" Joe shuddered, after diving in.

"What's the matter? Can't you take it?" Frank joked, splattering him with a sheet of water.

Ted Sewell roared with laughter as the taunt developed into a water duel between the two Hardys. Fleetfoot, meanwhile, was plunging and darting like an otter, coming up every now and then to shake his long, black hair out of his eyes.

After five minutes all of the boys were glad to hurry back on dry land, where they toweled themselves to a brisk glow. Having donned their clothes, they ate a quick meal. Then they embarked once more to continue their journey.

An hour later Fleetfoot paused in his paddling and pointed to stone boundary markers on both banks of the stream. "Now we in Canada," he told the others. "This where redcoats live."

"I guess you mean the Royal Canadian Mounted Police," Frank replied.

"That right," Fleetfoot said.

The boys scanned the forest with eager interest. Though now in mountain country, they were again entering an area of dense wilderness. Both banks of the river were heavily timbered and overgrown with tangled green underbrush.

"Guess they don't need an immigration office at a wilderness place like this," Joe remarked with a smile.

Several miles east of the boundary markers, the boys saw a screaming horde of birds wheeling and circling over the right bank of the river. Gulls, terns, and grebes filled the air with their raucous cries.

"Hey, there's a blue heron!" Joe exclaimed as the graceful creature rose above the treetops, flapping its wings.

"Why all the birds?" Frank wondered aloud.

"Must be a salmon spawning ground near," Ted conjectured.

"That right," Fleetfoot said. "We see it very soon."

Presently they reached a point where the right bank of the river opened into a shallow cove. The backwater was swarming with salmon. Trout and walleyes, too, could be seen darting among the shallows.

"Wow! A fisherman's paradise!" Joe gasped. "Chet should be here!"

Every few moments one of the birds flocking overhead would swoop down and seize a fish in its beak.

"Birds eat young salmon," Fleetfoot explained. "Other fish eat salmon eggs, too."

"It's a wonder any survive," Frank remarked.

"They do, though—millions of 'em," said Ted. "Old Mother Nature sees to that."

"Mother Nature and the Fish and Wildlife Service!" Joe remarked wryly.

The river became more and more shallow as they continued paddling upstream. Soon the canoes scraped the gravel bars that stretched from bank to bank.

"We make portage," Fleetfoot announced. "Near headwaters now."

"Wait a minute," Frank said slowly. He was gazing at what seemed to be a dried-up creek bed, branching off to the west. "Joe, do you remember those two bends in the river we passed back a ways?"

"Sure. Why?"

"I believe this may be the spot shown on the map in the knapsack we found. That had a line branching off above two loops, just like that dry creek over there."

Joe's eyes widened with recognition. "You're right, Frank!" he said excitedly. "I'll bet this is the place! And maybe this is the creek Jess Jenkins was talking about that leads to the grave houses!"

"Let's find out," Frank returned cautiously.

Beaching the canoes, the boys unloaded their gear and covered everything carefully with stones and brush. Then they struck inland. Much of the creek bed was filled with reeds and waist-high grass. Heavy timber lined both banks.

A mile of walking brought them to a wide clearing which was becoming overgrown.

"Look! There they are!" Joe cried out.

The grave houses which Jess had described stood at scattered points about the area.

"This is it, all right," Frank declared, grinning. "The Indian burial ground!" Most of the small log structures were half-rotten and falling apart with age.

"Come on! Let's see what's inside them!" Joe exclaimed. He ran to a rickety structure and stepped inside. "Oh!" he whispered. "Look at that!"

Frank, Ted, and Fleetfoot also stopped short and stared at the macabre spectacle. Gray, crumbling bones lay scattered beside a shallow open grave in the dirt floor. Fleetfoot stared at them fearfully. Then his eyes roved to a moldy wooden chest, which stood open nearby. It had apparently been lifted off the grave.

Joe glanced inside the chest and announced that it contained only a stone knife and a few small trinkets.

"Someone's been here before us," Frank muttered.

"Maybe this is one of the grave houses the prospectors looted back in Jess Jenkins' time," Joe suggested.

Frank shook his head. "I'm sure the grave hasn't been open that long."

One by one, they checked the other grave houses in the area. All had been rifled.

"Guess we're too late." Ted Sewell sighed.

"Maybe not," Joe said hopefully. "There's another one over there, among the trees. The door hasn't even been opened. Let's take a look."

The boys hurried over to inspect it, and found that the door gave way easily to the first blow from a rifle butt. Inside, the dirt floor was untouched, and on it was a wooden chest, similar to the first, falling to pieces with age. A few streaks of blue and red paint still clung to its rotting surface.

"Hurry! Open it!" Ted blurted out.

Frank whipped out his knife. As he inserted the blade under the lid, the others watched breathlessly, wondering what they would find inside.

CHAPTER XVII

Buried Treasure

THE LID of the old chest creaked as Frank pried it open. Then Joe let out a whistle of awe.

"Jumpin' fishhooks! Will you look at that!"

The chest was heaped with jade necklaces, copper arm bands, delicate ivory figures carved from walrus tusks, and Oriental bowls fashioned of hammered metal. The boys' eyes bulged as Frank scooped out piece after piece and held it up for inspection.

"I'll bet this stuff's worth a fortune!" Ted gasped.

"Museums would probably pay plenty for it," Frank agreed.

"Look!" Joe seized one of the jade trinkets. "It's the same bird that was carved on the piece we found in the knapsack."

"I guess that clinches our deduction about the treasure," Frank said, after carrying the piece out into the daylight so he could examine it more carefully. He added wryly, "We started out on this case as sleuths. But what with that dinosaur bone you spotted, Joe, this seems to be turning into a scientific expedition!"

Fenton Hardy had often impressed on his two sons their responsibility for safeguarding any valuables which turned up during a case. Remembering this, Joe asked, "Frank, what are we going to do with this treasure? We can't just leave 'em here."

"I agree," Frank said. "If we do, they may be stolen before the authorities can pick them up."

"Why not take the chest with us?" Ted asked.

"We might be robbed," Joe objected. "There's too much danger of a brush with the gang."

"Besides," Frank pointed out, "I doubt if we have the right to carry such treasure out of British Columbia, even if we planned to turn it over to the Canadian authorities later."

After discussing the problem from every angle, the boys decided to bury the chest somewhere away from the grave houses. Then, at the earliest possible opportunity, they would notify the Canadian Mounties of their find.

Both Joe and Frank still were concerned about the code message they had intercepted in the singing wilderness. In case any of the gang might be spying on them, they insisted on combing the

trees and brush around the burial ground. Even
Fleetfoot's keen eyes, however, failed to detect
any trace of an enemy.

Satisfied that no one but themselves had seen
the treasure, Frank chose a tall cedar as a marker
for their cache.

"This should be easy to find again," he said.
"It's much taller than any of the other trees
around here."

"Okay," said Ted. "Let's get the chest."

Joe and Fleetfoot, meanwhile, had started back
to the canoes to fetch a camp spade and some oilskin. When they returned, the boys dug a hole
alongside the cedar, wrapped the chest in oilskin,
and after burying it, carefully replaced the earth.
This they covered with brush.

Before leaving, Ted suggested that they make a
final search of the area to be certain there was no
grave house which they might have overlooked.

"Good idea," Joe said eagerly. "We might find
more treasure."

Fanning out on both sides of the creek bed, the
boys forced their way through the heavy thickets
and peered among the dense groves of evergreens.
A low call from Joe brought the others hurrying
to his side. He was standing at a point where the
forest thinned out into an area of semi-swampland.

"Look!" he pointed to the ground. The soft
earth showed a clear trail of footprints made by

several men. Two of the sets of prints showed the same circle-and-star heelmarks which the Hardys had seen before.

"The gang's been here all right," Frank said in a low voice.

Not far away was a trampled area which looked to the young sleuths as if it might have been the scene of a meeting. From this spot, most of the prints led back toward the river. One set of prints, however, headed off in a different direction.

"Let's follow this set," Frank suggested.

The boys proceeded cautiously, alert for any danger. Beyond the swamp area, the wilderness thickened again, with tangled underbrush pressing so closely on every side that single file became necessary.

Taking the lead, Joe pushed on through the dense thickets. Behind him came Fleetfoot, then Ted and Frank.

Presently the forest thinned out somewhat, and Joe halted in surprise. Just ahead, partly screened by the trees, stood a cabin.

Apparently the noise of crashing through the underbrush had been heard by the occupants, for the cabin door suddenly opened and a man burst out, pointing a rifle in their direction.

He had on the striped trousers and boots of the Royal Canadian Mounted Police, but instead of the regulation tunic, he wore a checkered sports shirt.

"Halt!" the man cried. "I see the three of you!
Don't move!"

Just then a second man appeared in the cabin
doorway. He was tall, bearded and emaciated, and
was trailing a chain from one ankle.

"Dad!" Ted gasped. "That other guy's no
Mountie—he's a phony!"

In his excitement Ted would have rushed forward, in spite of the uniformed man's leveled
rifle. Joe, however, grabbed his arm and held him
back.

In a low whisper Joe called to his brother, who
was still concealed from the view of the rifleman.
"Sneak up on him from the rear, Frank!"

Without another word, the older Hardy
dropped on his hands and knees, worked his way
back to denser cover, and made a circle of the
cabin. In a few minutes he approached it from
the rear as the gunman barked:

"Okay, you boy heroes! Move forward with
your hands high!"

By this time Frank was peering around the
corner of the cabin. Joe moved forward, very
slowly, giving his brother time to act.

"Come on, there!" the man cried angrily, "I
ain't got all day!"

Frank, meanwhile, tiptoed up behind the man,
hardly daring to breathe, lest he give himself away.
Joe, Ted, and Fleetfoot looked on tensely as they
approached, hands in the air.

Frank was now directly behind the phony Mountie!

"Ha—ha," the thug jeered. "The boss said I might get company. Now step— Ugh!"

The words choked off suddenly as Frank crooked one arm around the man's windpipe, and snatched the rifle away with the other. The man whirled and fought like a wildcat, but Frank wrestled him to the ground. Joe and Fleetfoot, rushing forward, quickly helped to subdue the scoundrel.

"All right! On your feet!" Frank snapped, stepping back and covering the "Mountie" with his own rifle. Muttering, the prisoner obeyed.

Ted, meanwhile, was having a joyful reunion with his father. "I can hardly believe it's you, son!" Mr. Sewell said huskily, as he and Ted hugged each other. "This is too good to be true!"

"It *is* true, Dad! And we'll soon have that chain off!"

Frank ordered the impostor to surrender the key to Joe, who quickly unlocked the shackle from around Mr. Sewell's ankle. The wildlife expert then told his story. He had discovered the same "singing wilderness" which the boys had come across later.

"I couldn't figure out who was broadcasting," Mr. Sewell related, "but I decided to report the matter to Juneau. Before I could do so, several men jumped me from behind. They brought me

"Halt!" the man ordered. "Don't move!"

upriver in a boat, and then marched me inland
to this cabin. I've been chained up here ever
since."

Frank wanted to ask if Mr. Sewell had heard
the gang mention anything about the lost moon
rocket, but decided against it. "No sense letting
our prisoner in on what we know," he thought.
Turning to Fleetfoot, he directed, "Take this fellow away from the cabin and keep him covered,
will you?" The Indian nodded, borrowed Ted's
rifle, and herded the captive out of earshot.

Then Frank turned back to Mr. Sewell. "We
believe this gang may be led by foreigners, but
that phony "Mountie" speaks like an American.
Any idea who he is?"

Mr. Sewell shook his head. "I don't even know
the fellow's name. The other men called him
'Watchdog.' However, from his accent, I'd say he
comes from Chicago!"

The Hardys gave Mr. Sewell a quick summary
of the whole case to date, including their finding
of the Indian treasure at the burial ground. The
woodsman was astounded, but could offer no solu-
tion to the mystery.

"The men who captured me were careful not
to say anything which might give me a clue," he
explained. "However, I once overheard them
mention the word 'totem.' "

"Meaning what, do you suppose?" Joe asked.
"A totem pole?"

"Probably so. Perhaps they're using one as a landmark."

"It may mark the spot where they've cached the loot from the Indian grave houses," Frank conjectured.

Ted's father had been fed little more than scraps of food during his captivity, and was obviously in need of nourishment. The boys, too, were growing extremely hungry, so they prepared a meal from the gang's supplies in the cabin.

Afterward, they started back toward the river with their prisoner. Twice during the trek Watchdog tried to escape, but each time the boys quickly forced him back on the trail.

They were halfway to the river when a strange, shrill birdcall suddenly shattered the silence of the forest.

"Hey! Where'd that come from?" Joe exclaimed as he and the others looked around, scanning the branches of the nearby trees.

Mr. Sewell was particularly puzzled. "I've never heard a birdcall like that!" he declared. "I wonder—"

His words broke off at a shout of dismay from Frank. "The prisoner! He's gone!"

CHAPTER XVIII

The Totem's Secret

FRANK and Joe glanced about in consternation. Watchdog had vanished as suddenly as the strange birdcall had stopped!

"Where'd he go?" asked Ted, bewildered by the unexpected turn in their luck.

"Search me," Joe replied sheepishly.

Frank now was red-faced with anger. "It was a trick! We were caught flat-footed!"

Mr. Sewell had to concur. "Watchdog is a ventriloquist," he told the chagrined boys. "He used to practice at the cabin to pass away the time."

"I get it!" Joe exclaimed. "He projected that birdcall, and while we were gawking around, he sneaked off!"

"And we fell for it," Ted said glumly.

But Fleetfoot seemed unperturbed. As everyone glanced about for a sign of their escaped captive, the Indian boy announced confidently, "Me find him." He scanned the bushes on all sides. The

Hardys looked too, but could find no sign of the fugitive.

Then suddenly Fleetfoot straightened up and pointed to the right. "Bad man go that way. See footprints."

The youth started off at a quick lope, Frank and Joe following at his heels. Ted and his father hurried along behind them. The searchers moved quietly, every sense alert.

"I hope Fleetfoot knows what he's doing," Frank said over his shoulder to Joe. "This might be a plan by the gang to ambush all of us."

As he spoke, the Indian boy stopped and raised his right hand. The searchers came to a halt. Fleetfoot beckoned them forward and pointed to a massive rock formation which loomed up on one side of a creek bed. At the foot of it was a black, gaping hole, obviously the entrance to a cave.

"Is that where he went?" Frank asked. The Indian boy showed his white teeth in a smile that said "Yes."

"How are we going to flush him?" Ted wanted to know.

Frank was worried that the cave might have an exit as well. "I'll scout around back of those rocks to see if there's a way out."

Frank had gone only three feet when a hoarse cry emitted from the opening in the rocks! The eerie sound made the hair stand up on the back of Joe's neck. Even Fleetfoot was startled.

The weird cry issued forth again. Frank and Joe screwed up their courage and advanced closer to the black hole.

All at once the head and shoulders of a man appeared. Crawling on all fours, he scrambled out of the cave like a beaten animal.

"Watchdog!" Frank yelled.

The fugitive sprang to his feet and rushed forward in headlong flight. As Frank and Joe converged upon him, Watchdog tripped on a root and fell violently to the ground with a thud.

"Got you!" Frank cried. He grasped Watchdog's arms and held them behind his back.

Then, just as suddenly, Frank sprang off his prisoner. "Whew!" he exclaimed, sniffing. "Skunk!"

"How right you are!" Joe made a face and held his nose.

In spite of the gravity of the situation, everyone except the prisoner, who lay half stunned and gasping for breath, burst out laughing.

"There comes friend!" Fleetfoot pointed to the cave entrance. A small black animal with a white streak down his back poked his nose out, looked about disdainfully, and walked off sedately into the underbrush.

"Mr. Polecat deserves a medal!" Joe said, doubling over with mirth.

"But what about Watchdog?" Ted grinned. "How can we travel with a smell like that?"

Hearing his name, the prisoner pulled himself up to a sitting position and glanced groggily about.

"You—you got to help me," he said weakly. "I can't wear these duds any longer."

"Come on. A bath will do it," Frank said. He and Joe led Watchdog to a nearby creek.

"Jump in," Frank ordered, unable to suppress a wry smile. "Clothes and all."

Watchdog obliged. He dived into the water and splashed about, at the same time emitting uncomplimentary remarks both about the skunk and his captors.

"Be careful what you say," Joe called, obviously enjoying the thug's discomfiture. "Or we'll put you back in that cave."

"I'll get even for this." Watchdog glowered, as he stepped from the creek and wrung the water from his clothes.

"We didn't plant the skunk there," Ted needled their prisoner.

Mr. Sewell could not suppress a grin as he added, "You certainly picked the wrong hiding place!"

Frank then turned to their prisoner. "Just to see that you don't try any more tricks, we'll keep you close to us!"

"Hey, not too close," Joe begged, as Frank pulled off his belt and tied Watchdog's hands securely behind him.

"Now listen," Frank told him sternly, "we'll travel single file. You stay five paces behind me—Joe, you keep about the same distance behind this guy."

Anxious not to lose any more time, the group proceeded to the river at a brisk pace. Here the canoes were uncovered and reloaded. Frank retrieved his belt while Joe rebound the prisoner's hands with rope. Then he was placed in the bottom of one of the canoes and covered with a piece of tarpaulin, in case other members of his gang should appear along the way.

"We ought to report what's happened," Joe said. "Do you think we can raise Juneau on the radio?"

Frank set to work immediately, but after hoisting the aerial, he could get only static over his headset.

"Terrific interference," he told Joe. "Sounds as if there's some electrical device here in the woods."

"Like what?" Ted asked.

"Perhaps someone else has a powerful radio," Mr. Sewell put in.

Joe winked at his brother. "Maybe a dentist has an office nearby," he said.

Frank gave his brother a thump on the arm. "Stow the corny jokes, brother!"

The lighthearted attitude of the Hardys continued after they had launched their canoe into the stream. With Ted and his father paddling alongside them, Frank and Joe fairly shot along with the rapid current.

"Boy, this is what I call fun!" Joe exulted as they sped through the foaming rapids.

A short time later Joe cried out, "Good-by Canada. Hello, Alaska!"

They crossed the boundary line at a rapid clip and mile after mile went by under the swift stroke of their paddles. At seven o'clock they beached their canoes long enough to eat supper.

"Frank," Joe said, his eyes dancing, "you can hand feed Skunkie Boy over there. I wouldn't advise untying him again."

"I caught him, so I guess I'm stuck with him." Frank grinned and moved over to where the prisoner lay in the canoe.

"Sit up," Frank said. "I'll feed you your beans. Watch your manners."

Watchdog chewed glumly as Frank fed him his supper.

"If you want room service during the night," Frank jested, "just push the button."

The sinister outline of Devil's Paw looming in the distance, however, brought the boys back to awareness of their grim situation.

"Are we going to camp here tonight?" Ted queried.

After a hasty conference, both the Hardys and Mr. Sewell decided against such a move.

"We ought to get our prisoner back safely to Juneau as soon as possible," the woodsman suggested.

Frank and Joe agreed. "Suppose you and Ted take him along," Frank said.

"And leave you here?"

"The three of us will be safe enough," he assured the Sewells.

Joe declared that they should at least stop at the enemy's camp long enough to see whether Robbie had returned to the helicopter.

"All right," Mr. Sewell acceded. "Ted and I will go on and report everything that has happened, but be careful, won't you?"

It was still daylight by the time the adventurers re-embarked and reached the point on the west bank of the river near the trail which led to the camp at Devil's Paw. Here the Hardys made another attempt to get in touch with Juneau by radio. This time the static was even louder.

"Boy! This is a real mystery!" Joe removed his headphones. "We're getting interference from something mighty powerful."

The Sewells stopped along the riverbank to say good-by, then paddled out of sight along the foaming river. After they had gone, Frank, Joe, and Fleetfoot turned their attention to the job of caching the two remaining canoes and their supplies.

Joe suggested that they also check on the fuel cans which they had hidden earlier. They found

them still in place and Fleetfoot reported no footprints were in evidence nearby.

Once again the three companions followed the
beaten trail up the mountainside to the camp.
Dodging behind the trees and peering from be-
neath the bushes, the boys silently approached
the area. Nobody was in sight.

Suddenly Joe clutched his brother's arm. "Look
over there," he said.

"What do you know about that? Robbie's
sweater!"

The three boys stepped forward to examine it.
It was a blue garment with red trim. The way it
lay on the ground, however, made Frank suspect
that it had not been casually dropped.

"Look!" he said, and indicated the left arm of
the sweater. "See how the sleeve is pointing, Joe."

"That was done on purpose!"

"Of course. Robbie put this here to give us directions."

Fleetfoot spoke up approvingly. "Robbie like
good Indian. He give sign."

The sweater arm pointed southwest over an
area of rock and shale. The ground was too hard
to reveal any footprints.

Frank and Joe left the sweater untouched as a
safety precaution, in case they lost their way and
wanted to find the trail again. Then they set off
with Fleetfoot. Gradually the ground sloped away
to a heavily wooded valley. Just before the edge of

the timber, Fleetfoot's keen eyes noted several sets of footprints heading in their general direction.

"We go right way," he said.

With extreme caution, the three boys pushed their way among the pines and underbrush. The forest was wrapped in a brooding silence. The setting sun shone blood red over the hills.

The Hardys and their Indian friend continued on through the towering trees. Frank was the first to step out into a small clearing. Silently he beckoned to the others.

"What's the matter?" said Joe, whispering into his brother's ear.

"Over there, next to that leaning pine tree."

Joe cupped his hands over his eyes to keep out the sun's glare.

"By golly, Frank, that's a thunderbird!"

The figure stood out above the tall grass and when Fleetfoot saw it, he said, "It top of totem pole."

Advancing cautiously, the boys came upon a ten-foot post, with angry-looking faces of salmon, bears, and sea otters with bared fangs.

At the top of the totem, a thunderbird leered down at them with outspread wings. Though badly weather-beaten, the pole still showed traces of red, yellow, and blue paint.

Frank and Joe discussed their find in muted voices.

"Could the pole be just a landmark?" Joe wanted to know.

"I'm sure it's more than that," Frank reasoned, "because the footprints led directly to it. This thunderbird totem must be of some special importance."

The Indian boy's hands were already moving over the carved images. He turned to grin at his two companions. "Sometime totem pole hide important message." Fleetfoot next felt around the indented mouth of the salmon.

"No message here," he said, disappointed.

Joe glanced up. "What about the thunderbird? Could that have a message in it?"

Fleetfoot shrugged. Whereupon Joe said, "Come on, Frank, give me a boost, I'll take a look for myself."

Frank cupped his hands together waist-high, and Joe placed his right foot in the hand stirrup.

"Up you go!" Frank gave Joe a strong boost.

Joe deftly put a foot on either of his brother's shoulders. He was now high enough to reach the thunderbird.

"Look in the beak," Fleetfoot said.

"False alarm," Joe reported. "The bird doesn't have a message and— Hey! Look out, Frank! Don't wiggle like that!"

His brother had moved slightly to slap at a mosquito, and in doing so had thrown Joe off balance. He pitched to one side, brushing against the right wing of the thunderbird. It fell off. "Look out, be-low!" Joe cried out. He hit the ground with a thud. The wing just missed his head.

"You hurt?" Fleetfoot asked.

"I'm all right," Joe said, getting up and rub-bing his thigh. "But look at the totem pole. I guess I've ruined it."

The three boys glanced up to the place where the wing had been ripped off the towering figure.

Fleetfoot looked surprised, "That meant to come off. Look! Hole in totem pole!"

"Jumping salmon!" Joe exclaimed. "Let's take a look."

This time Frank was hoisted to the shoulders of Joe and the Indian boy, who stood side by side. Tense with excitement, Frank planted his feet firmly on their shoulders, then on tiptoe, reached up into the opening.

"Hey, fellows!" he cried out. "There's some-thing in here!"

CHAPTER XIX

Enmeshed

JOE and Fleetfoot stared upward as Frank withdrew his hand from the opening in the totem pole.

"What did you find?" Joe called.

"A canvas sack. And is it heavy!"

When Frank had pulled the large sack free of the hole, he leaped nimbly to the ground with it. Then, quickly unloosening the drawstring, he dumped the bag's contents onto the ground.

"Look at that!" Joe cried out. "More treasure!"

"From grave houses!" Fleetfoot declared instantly. He picked up several of the ornaments and examined them curiously.

Frank spoke up. "Joe, this stuff must be priceless! I'll bet there's nothing like it, even in the Alaska Historical Museum!"

Joe reflected for a moment. "Do you suppose

161

Robbie pointed his sweater this way to lead us to the thunderbird's cache?"

"I doubt it," Frank said. "Robbie was probably interested only in where he was going—or being taken."

"And we don't know where that is yet." Joe's voice held a determined ring.

"Treasure or no," Frank said, "Robbie's safety is more important."

"What'll we do with this stuff, Frank? Carry it with us?"

"No, it's too heavy."

Fleetfoot had a suggestion. "We bury this, too, like other stuff. But first we must put back thunderbird's wing."

Standing on Frank's shoulder, Joe quickly replaced the wing, covering the opening in the totem as it was before. Fleetfoot, meanwhile, had found a cleft between two rocks. The boys laid their new treasure in the depression, covering it with a layer of brush, then a rotted tree limb which lay nearby.

With the artifacts concealed, the three companions trekked on, following the same direction as before. Ten minutes later Frank, in the lead, came upon a sapling with the lower branch freshly broken. "Fleetfoot! Joe! Look here! A marker!"

"You right," the Indian said, admiring his friend's knowledge of woodcraft.

"This means a change of direction, doesn't it?" Joe asked.

"Exactly," Frank replied. "Robbie was on his toes, all right."

Judging from the sticky sap which still oozed from the wound in the branch, the Hardy boys deduced that it had been broken only a short time before.

"We'd better be quieter than ever," Frank warned.

The boys alternated in taking the lead as they pushed through the dense underbrush. Intently they tried to avoid stepping on twigs and fallen branches so as not to betray their presence.

As they topped a low rise of ground, Fleetfoot motioned the Hardys to stop and listen. The brothers put their ears to the ground.

"Someone's walking up ahead," Frank whispered.

"Yes. Many feet," the Indian said. "We must be careful."

Creeping forward on knees and elbows, Frank, Joe, and Fleetfoot inched to the top of the knoll. There, completely hidden by foliage, they looked down into a little ravine. Below them was a group of men going through mysterious motions!

"One, two, four—six of them," Joe counted to himself.

In their hands all of the men held long poles

which they were moving back and forth over the ground and bushes.

Frank leaned close to his brother. "Mine detectors!" he exclaimed in a whisper.

"No wonder our radio's been full of static!" Joe whispered back. "These birds must have been pretty close to us all the time."

Frank touched Fleetfoot on the shoulder and motioned for him to withdraw. The three boys ducked below the brow of the hill. In an undertone Frank quickly explained the situation to Fleetfoot.

"It's the moon rocket they're looking for all right," he said.

"And it's not dark yet," Joe remarked. "They must be getting desperate to find it."

The brothers quizzed the Indian boy on whether he had seen the men use these mine detectors the night he crossed the river to investigate the flickering lights.

"No use them then," Fleetfoot replied.

"But where's Robbie?" Joe whispered. "You don't suppose they've—"

"I don't think they'd harm him," Frank said. "Robbie is their ace in the hole—they might need him in case they have to escape by helicopter."

"We'd better take a closer look," Joe suggested.

"Follow me," Fleetfoot said.

Depending on their Indian friend's acute sense of direction, the boys hunched low and crept after

him in a circuitous route which led down to one
end of the ravine. Then, darting from tree to tree
in the deepening evening shadows, the three boys
approached nearer to the six men.

Joe put his mouth close to his brother's ear.
"I'll bet you they're foreigners."

However, both he and Frank were startled
when one of the men straightened up and leaned
on his detector. "What a wild-goose chase!" the
man said. He wore khaki trousers and shirt to
match, open at the neck. A dark-green woodsman's cap was pulled low over his eyes.

"Yeah," another man said. "It doesn't make
sense. What could they drop out of an airplane
that was so valuable?"

"Oh, them foreigners don't give you any an-
swers," a third man spoke up. "They're pretty
clever, and after all, they're payin' us enough."

"Not enough to keep this poor guy tied up," another of their members called from across the
glen. Then he sang out, "Say how are you, skipper?"

A voice sounded from behind a large tree ten
yards ahead of the Hardys. "Let me go, will you,
fellows? Maybe I can help you out of the mess
you're in."

"Robbie!" Frank whispered.

"And these fellows are Americans!" Joe said.
"I don't get it! Where did the foreigners go?"

"I don't know that," his brother replied. "But

I believe these men are working for the gang. Maybe we can persuade them to come over on our side."

Fleetfoot, who had pressed close to the brothers, whispered, "No. Don't do that. These men no good. Loafers. Hang around dock at Ketchikan."

Frank and Joe decided to take their friend's advice. Even though the men who were scouring the woods with the mine detectors might not be out-and-out criminals, still the capture of the Hardys might be a feather in their cap.

"They might even hold us for ransom," Joe said.

Frank thought they could free Robbie and make a getaway by stealth. Fortunately, the six searchers moved farther from the spot where the captive pilot sat.

"Easy now!" Joe cautioned the others. "Don't scare Robbie. He might yell!"

The three companions inched along the ground, using every blade of tall grass as cover until they came up behind the tree from which Robbie's voice had emanated.

"Robbie! *Robbie!*" Frank whispered hoarsely.

"Wha—!"

"*Sh!*"

But Robbie's startled outcry had alerted the fellow with the green cap. "What'd you say, skipper?"

"Why don't you let me go?" Robbie called back promptly. Then in a hushed voice, he added, "Frank, Joe! Is that you?"

"Yes," Frank whispered. "Be quiet. We're trying to get you out of here."

Frank peered around the side of the tree. Robbie's hands were tied behind his back and his ankles were bound with leather thongs.

"Lie down," Frank said, "and stretch out as if you're taking a nap."

Robbie did as he was instructed, holding his wrists and ankles close to the sides of the tree. In the dim light the hands of Frank and Joe were barely visible as they reached around to cut the bonds of the helicopter pilot.

Robbie moved his arms and legs slowly so as to regain circulation. This accomplished, he slithered around the tree, unnoticed by the gang. Then, with the tree as a shield, he stood up. Fleetfoot motioned the three to follow and they set off at a rapid pace through the underbrush.

At first Robbie had difficulty keeping up with the boys because of cramps in his legs. These, however, were soon worked out as he jogged swiftly along beside his rescuers.

Now the boys were breathing hard as they hurried through the tangled woods. Part of the story of what had happened came out when, panting, the four stopped for a short rest.

"They haven't discovered you're missing yet,"

Joe said. Then he added, "Who are those fellows, Robbie?"

"Renegades from down the coast somewhere. They're working for those foreigners. Oh, I'd like to get my hands on that guy who kidnaped me!"

"What was his name?" asked Frank.

"Remus—or something like that."

"Remo Stransky!" Frank exclaimed, recalling his hunch.

"You were right," Joe said. "How did he get away with it?" he asked the pilot.

"Pushed a gun in my back just as I was about to take off for the glacier to pick up you boys."

"But what about the package dropped to us by the airplane?" Joe asked, perplexed.

"Remo bragged that a friend would do that," Robbie told them, "just to throw you off the trail."

"Did you write the note?"

"Yes. I was forced to."

Now Fleetfoot spoke up. "You know what these men look for?"

"No. Not exactly. Something very important."

Robbie told them that his foreign captors insisted that one of their country's airplanes had dropped valuable cargo by mistake. The United States government wouldn't co-operate in helping them find it, they had claimed. "So," concluded Robbie, "they decided to take matters into their own hands."

"What a phony story!" Joe declared. "I'll bet a riverful of salmon they're looking for that moon rocket."

Just then shouts of angry men echoed through the darkening woods.

"They've found out you've escaped!" said Frank. "Come on! Let's go!"

Like a slender brown ghost, Fleetfoot led them racing through the woodlands along a trail barely perceptible in the gloom. Five minutes later the cries of their pursuers were lost in the distance.

"We've shaken them," Joe said.

"Don't be too sure," his brother cautioned. He turned to Robbie. "Do they have a radio?"

"Yes. A strong sending set."

"Then they'll report this to Stransky," Frank said. "We've got to be extra careful."

The four jogged along at an easier pace and the helicopter pilot told more of his story. "The foreign gang, hunting for this lost valuable in the woodlands, had come upon the Indian grave houses and rifled them."

Robbie related that he did manage to drop his sweater and break the tree branch to mark the trail without his captors noticing. "They got careless about watching me," he went on. "Too busy looking for a spot to stash the loot."

Frank interrupted. "They found it—in the thunderbird totem."

Robbie was amazed. "How'd you find out?"

The Hardys gave him a brief account of Joe's accidental discovery. The gang, Robbie said, had also come upon the hiding place by chance. "And that salmon-poaching business," he added, "was just a cover-up for this giant search."

The flier was delighted to hear that the boys had brought cans of aviation fuel and cached them near the riverbank.

"We'll be there soon," Frank declared.

It was decided that the boys would leave their canoes, as well as the treasure, hidden, and take off with Robbie in the helicopter.

"Now that we know where these fellows are," he said, "a flying police detail can help us round them up."

Skirting Devil's Paw at a safe distance, the four made their way down the steep slope toward Robbie's helicopter. The moon had come up, and cast a luminous glow on the sides of the craft.

"Well, here she is safe and sound," Robbie said, putting his foot on a rung at the side of the helicopter. He was just about to lift himself up to the cabin when a sudden swishing sound filled the air. Frank, Joe, and Fleetfoot, poised behind the pilot, whirled about.

"Look out, Frank!" Joe called as he saw the dim figures of five men leap suddenly out from the shadow of a boulder.

At the same time a large fish net fell over the heads and shoulders of Frank and the Indian boy!

CHAPTER XX

Aerial Roundup

WITH cries and whoops the five attackers rushed upon the boys. Frank and Fleetfoot, entangled in the net, could offer little resistance as the assailants fought to subdue Joe and Robbie. Both retaliated furiously, but the odds were insurmountable.

In five minutes all four companions lay exhausted on the ground. Their hands had been tied behind them by the gloating victors.

As one of the gang examined the bonds, he rasped in English, "Nice work with the net, Igor. We got 'em all. Herd 'em together and tie the seine around the bunch. We have our fish."

"Remo Stransky!" Joe lunged out at him, but in vain. Stransky stepped back and laughed in the youth's face.

"Save your strength!" he taunted. "This seine is made of your American nylon and is quite unbreakable."

"You won't get away with this," Frank cried out.

"Ah, we will." Stransky's lips curled gloatingly. "You Hardys and your two foolish friends here will never leave the forest alive to warn the police!"

"Don't be too sure of that!" Frank gritted. "Whatever happens to us, Stransky, you and your gang will be caught."

The foreign ringleader threw back his head and laughed harshly. "I'll say this much for you Hardys, you never give up. I realize that you and your helpers have found out a great deal, too much in fact, but understand this, my countrymen and I will not be cheated of success!"

The Hardys, Robbie, and Fleetfoot were searched and their hunting knives taken away.

"We'll relieve you of these," Stransky said with a sneer. "So you can't cut your way to freedom." Then he spoke into a small walkie-talkie handed to him by one of his henchmen.

"Okay, my American allies," he said. "We have snared the Hardys and the others. You will get a bonus for this." Then he added, "Keep on looking there until I instruct you further."

Stransky turned to his captives. "Come now," he said, prodding Frank. "We have no time to waste."

To his henchmen, Stransky gave crisp orders. Two of them immediately jerked the prisoners around and headed them toward the trail leading up to the Devil's Paw camp. The boys stumbled along. Once Robbie fell to the ground and was roughly yanked to his feet. Straining and sweating, he and the boys were half dragged, half shoved along the rocky trail. It was dark by the time they reached the camp, where the four captives were pushed to the ground.

Stransky spoke again into the walkie-talkie. "Assemble at camp, men!"

Frank and Joe, though most uncomfortable, welcomed the opportunity to lie down. Huddled with Fleetfoot and Robbie, they were parched and hungry.

"This is outrageous!" Robbie muttered. Struggling to his feet, he thrashed about in a vain attempt to break the nylon strands.

"Calm yourself," Stransky called out with a hoarse laugh. Then he directed one of his men, "Guard them closely, so they don't escape while we prepare supper."

The guard, who spoke English, as well as Stransky's native tongue, stretched down on the ground beside the prisoners. He taunted the Hardys. "I understand you found the boss's knapsack. A lot of good it did you!"

"How did you know that?" Frank asked.

"One of our spies in Juneau found out." The guard laughed raucously. "Fish! Salmon in the seine! Ha—ha—ha!"

"You'll laugh out of the other side of your mouth," Joe muttered. "Just wait."

"Quiet!"

"What do you intend to do with us?" Frank asked.

"What usually happens to unwanted fish?" the fellow taunted with obvious enjoyment of the Hardys' discomfort. "You throw them into the ocean." Then he chortled and relaxed in the high grass.

His compatriots, meanwhile, had started a roaring campfire. The light flickered over the faces of the four prisoners who reclined glumly in the shadow of some tall bushes.

About twenty minutes later the sound of many footsteps crashing through the woods brought the Hardys alert.

"Joe! Maybe it's a rescue party!" Frank said.

But the boys were doomed to disappointment, for into the circle of firelight stepped the gang's American henchmen carrying their mine detectors.

"So you caught 'em, eh?" said the man with the green cap.

"Yeah," another chuckled. "I hear those Hardys are just a couple of amateur detectives."

"Boy, I wish Dad were here now," Joe thought, furious. "We'd show 'em who are amateurs."

To add to the misery of the trapped quartet, their captors brought a steaming tin of stew to the guard. The aroma wafted to their nostrils, causing their mouths to water. But they remained silent, determined to ask no favors.

Soon the group around the campfire were eating and joking loudly.

"Now that the Hardys and their friends are tied up," Stransky said, "we can go ahead in our search without any more trouble from those interlopers."

"What about the reinforcements, boss?"

"They're on the way," Stransky replied. "They'll skip past Prito and his fat friend tonight. With ten more fellows helping, you should find that—er—lost cargo in no time."

Frank and Joe exchanged glances of alarm. If they could only warn Chet and Tony of the impending peril! "It looks as if it's curtains for all of us!" Joe whispered glumly. The Hardys' hope was fading like the flickering flames of the campfire.

With the meal over, the captives and their guard were swallowed up in the shadows. Frank had even started to doze when suddenly he was snapped to consciousness by the sudden sound of:

Oomph!

Startled, the Hardys saw to their astonishment that it was their guard who had uttered the sound! This was followed by the crack of fist meeting jaw. Then there was silence. Frank and Joe, as well as Robbie and Fleetfoot, stared into the gloom.

Suddenly a voice close to them whispered, "How're you fellows? All right?"

"Chet!" Frank gasped in disbelief. "Are you alone?"

"No, I'm here too," came another voice.

"Tony!" Joe said in muffled but joyful tones.

"Well, we took care of that guy for a while," said Chet. "I jumped on his middle, then Tony socked him."

"Sure good see you!" Fleetfoot said.

"You bet!" Robbie spoke up. "Hope you brought a sharp knife."

"Right here. I'll have you out in a jiffy." Tony glanced quickly at the men about the campfire. Some were now asleep, others were lolling about. Desultory chatter muffled the sound of Tony's knife as it cut through the strands of the seine.

"There," he said finally. "You're free. Let's get out of here."

"Where to?" asked Chet.

"Robbie's copter," replied Frank. "I think we can make it this time."

Tony held out a small compass attached to his belt. The luminous face gave the group their bearings. Then, with Fleetfoot in the lead, the six stealthily crept away.

Keeping tensely on the alert for signs of detection from the enemy, they proceeded for some time in dead silence. Finally, feeling they were safely out of earshot, Joe asked Chet and Tony, "How'd you find us, fellows?"

"Easy," Tony said. "We spotted that campfire a mile away."

As the boys walked on, Chet told Frank and Joe how they had become worried about their friends' long absence.

"Tony got half a dozen guards as replacements to take charge at the island," he added, "so we could come to look for you."

Frank slapped the stout boy affectionately on the shoulder. Chet's loyalty was unswerving.

Once Fleetfoot had found the slope leading to the helicopter, the party cautiously traversed the rocky terrain. Frank and Joe, with the aid of Tony and Chet, carried the cans of gasoline from their hiding place. Reaching the helicopter, they fueled it. Robbie, meanwhile, checked the instrument panel, as Fleetfoot looked on with awe.

"Me get whirlybird ride now?" the Indian boy asked.

"Right!" Joe said. "You certainly deserve it!"

Preparations for the flight went on under mounting tension. Every few moments Frank or Joe glanced up at the rocky cliff to see whether or not Stransky's men were pursuing them.

Finally Robbie announced, "Okay, fellows, we're set to go, but I've got bad news."

"What's that?" Joe said.

"I can't take all of you out in one trip. Two must be left behind."

"I'll stay," Joe volunteered.

"Me too," offered Chet without hesitation.

Frank protested at first, saying he wanted to stay with his brother. But Joe insisted that Frank go back to give details of their adventure.

With snappy salutes, Chet and Joe bade their companions farewell. The door of the helicopter closed. With a whining sound, the rotors turned, at first slowly, then whirring into action.

Suddenly, above the noise of the rotors, Joe and Chet heard a volley of rifleshots ring out from the cliff.

"Run for cover!" Joe cried out.

The two boys darted behind a boulder. "Will the copter get off in time?" Joe wondered, his heart pounding. The lives of Frank and the three others aboard were at stake! Breathlessly, Joe and Chet watched as the helicopter rose, gained sufficient altitude, and took forward flight. The lights of rifle fire still winked on the brow of the cliff. In return, the helicopter blinked its running lights.

"Thank goodness!" Joe exclaimed. "They're safe!"

In the helicopter, meanwhile, Robbie had worked feverishly to get out of range of the snipers. Their first warning of enemy fire had been a bullet ripping through the fuselage close to Frank's head.

Now beyond reach of the foreigners' guns, Frank, Tony, and Robbie conferred. "Better contact Juneau pronto," Frank said.

"Right!" Robbie flicked on the radio.

It took only a few minutes to relay the urgent summons. The operator at the seaplane base promised to alert the proper authorities, not only in the state of Alaska, but also in British Columbia.

"Now what?" Tony asked.

"We'll stand by," Frank replied. "Shouldn't take long."

His conjecture proved correct. In a matter of minutes fighter aircraft of both the United States and Canadian forces came streaking low over the woods. Robbie had pinpointed their location.

As if by magic, it suddenly turned daylight as powerful magnesium flares attached to parachutes lighted the entire area. This was followed by more billowing chutes—paratroopers! They ringed the area and their walkie-talkie reports could be heard plainly over the radio of the hovering helicopter.

The action was swift and conclusive. A few scattered bursts of machine-gun fire, and the troops had rounded up the entire gang.

"Good show. Better than cowboy movie!" Fleetfoot exclaimed.

The others laughed. Then Frank urged, "Let's get an Army helicopter to go down with us and pick up Joe and Chet."

Robbie radioed the request and received an affirmative reply.

"We'll stand by to follow you in," came the Army pilot's voice.

With rotors whirling, Robbie set his craft down at the place where they had left the two boys. Magnesium flares still drifting down from the sky illuminated the area. Finally Chet and Joe dashed out from between two large boulders. They reached the helicopter as the Army craft came in alongside.

"Frank!" Joe called excitedly as his brother jumped down from the helicopter. "We found it! We found it!"

"What?" Frank asked, running up.

"The moon rocket! It made a crater just beyond the place where we were hiding."

Joe and Chet led the others to the spot. Only part of the metal tube could be seen protruding from the sandy spot where the rocket had landed.

"This is it all right!" Robbie declared as he examined the words etched into the tube's smooth surface.

Moments later, a colonel from the Air Force joined the boys. When told about the find, he quickly swore them all to secrecy.

"You've all done your country a tremendous

service," he praised the Hardys and their friends, then hastened off to radio a coded report to Washington.

A little later Robbie's group took off in his helicopter, while Joe and Chet boarded the Army helicopter for the ride back to Juneau.

"Wow, what excitement!" Joe exclaimed as he sat down.

At the moment Joe had no way of knowing that more excitement was to come the Hardys' way very soon. In their next adventure, **THE MYSTERY OF THE CHINESE JUNK**, the two young sleuths are plunged into danger when they try to find the key to a baffling puzzle.

The Hardy boys and their friends rendezvoused at the air base in Juneau. There, they learned that Remo's reinforcements had been captured at the mouth of the Kooniak. Frank and Joe quickly put through a radio message to their father in Bayport and took turns telling of their adventures.

"I'm mighty proud of you boys," Fenton Hardy said, after hearing the full story. "Are you going back for the buried treasure?"

"Tomorrow, Dad."

Just then, Tony Prito brought in more news, which was relayed by Frank to Bayport. The prisoner, nicknamed "Watchdog," had finally confessed to police that his real name was Shad Yawke. He had been hired by the Stranskys to terrorize the stream guard on duty in the Kooniak.

He had also hired the salmon poachers to mislead the Hardys, in case they should guess the foreign ring's true purpose—that of finding the moon rocket.

Yawke confirmed Frank's suspicion about the star-heel imprint which the boys had found in so many places. It was the trade-mark of a foreign manufacturer whose shoes were worn by the alien gang.

"A stupid oversight by the Stranskys," Joe commented.

The captured henchman admitted, too, the hurling of the fire bomb and the looting of the Indian grave houses by the gang. Further grilling revealed that he knew about the ancient Indian paddle. One of the gang had taken the blade and subsequently lost it when spying on Tony Prito.

Mr. Hardy supplied his sons with additional information about Romo Stransky's activities.

"When Romo learned from his twin that Tony was sending for you boys," Mr. Hardy related, "he started buying all those plane seats."

"And was he the truck driver who forced us off the road?"

"Yes."

"Well, I guess that clears up the mystery, Dad. We'll be home soon." Frank said good-by and hung up.

At that moment Chet walked into the radio room, his face beaming bright as an airplane beacon. "There's one thing I didn't tell you fellows about."

"What's that? Did you dig up some more crooks, Chet?" Frank asked with a twinkle.

"No," the boy said. "I caught a salmon, a twenty-pound beaut. We're going to have a real feast tonight. Fleetfoot will cook it Indian style."

Frank and Joe chuckled. "Here's one time I'm with you," Joe said, pumping the stout boy's hand. "I'm hungry."

"Me too!" Frank agreed heartily.

"Call the fellows together." Joe grinned. "This'll be one salmon the Alaskan bears won't get!"